Praise for *The Dating Games #1: First Date*

"Forget about The Hunger Games! *The Dating Games # 1: First Date*, by Melody Carlson, is the new series to which you should be drawn."

—*The Celebrity Cafe*

"Not all characters are religious, but all love and respect their parents and sincerely try to form real friendships even when jealousy strikes. It's all completely innocent and will be a welcome book for those uncomfortable with more frank fiction for teens. Perfect for young Christian readers and fine for others too."

—*Kirkus Reviews*

"Questions about friendship and Christian values are presented realistically but not overwhelmingly, and teen readers will be entertained by the drama and excitement. . . . A fast read and amusing story that ends with more adventures to come."

—*RT Book Reviews*

Praise for *The Dating Games #2: Blind Date*

"Cassidy, Emma, Bryn, Abby, and Devon continue to be quite a diverse group of friends who often delve into frenemy territory, creating stress and drama that mirrors the teenage experience. Their struggle over how to treat Devon when she takes steps in a negative direction demonstrates how we should be forgiving and patient in imitation of Christ."

—*RT Book Reviews*, 4 stars

"I always say it, but Melody's grip on teens and the way they think astounds me every time."

—*Christian Manifesto*

the
dating
games #3:

Double Date

Books by Melody Carlson

Devotions for Real Life
Just Another Girl
Anything but Normal
Never Been Kissed
Allison O'Brian on Her Own—Volume 1
Allison O'Brian on Her Own—Volume 2
Double Take
A Simple Song
My Amish Boyfriend
Trading Secrets

LIFE AT KINGSTON HIGH

The Jerk Magnet
The Best Friend
The Prom Queen

THE DATING GAMES

The Dating Games #1: First Date
The Dating Games #2: Blind Date
The Dating Games #3: Double Date

c.2

the
dating
games #3:

Double Date

MELODY CARLSON

Revell

a division of Baker Publishing Group
Grand Rapids, Michigan

© 2015 by Melody Carlson

Published by Revell
a division of Baker Publishing Group
P.O. Box 6287, Grand Rapids, MI 49516-6287
www.revellbooks.com

Printed in the United States of America

Library of Congress Cataloging-in-Publication Data
Carlson, Melody.
    The Dating Games. #3 Double date / Melody Carlson.
        pages cm.
        Summary: "The Dating Games club is ready to expand—but can they agree on who their new members will be?"— Provided by publisher.
        ISBN 978-0-8007-2129-9 (pbk.)
        [1. Dating (Social customs—Fiction. 2. Clubs—Fiction. 3. Friendship—Fiction. 4. High schools—Fiction. 5. Schools—Fiction. 6. Christian life—Fiction.] I. Title. II. Title: Double date.
    PZ7.C216637
    [Fic]—dc23   2014030733

The author is represented by Sara A. Fortenberry Literary Agency.

15   16   17   18   19   20   21   7   6   5   4   3   2   1

By Monday morning, Cassidy Banks had some serious doubts about Felicia Ruez. She hated feeling like this, considering how much Emma seemed to like this girl and the fact that the Dating Games club (aka the DG) had recently voted to induct Felicia. Unfortunately, Cassidy's concerns over Felicia had to do with character issues. Or more specifically, Felicia's *reputation*. To be fair, Cassidy rarely paid attention to school gossip, but the stories she'd heard lately seemed to be jiving with this new image that Felicia was presenting.

Cassidy was the first to admit that of all the girls in the DG, she was by far the most conservative. Especially when it came to appearances. Thanks to her average good looks—her long, no-nonsense brown hair and brown eyes, her addiction to blue jeans and hoodies, and her general dislike of cosmetics— she knew she wasn't exactly a showstopper. Despite her low-maintenance beauty habits, it hadn't escaped her notice that

Felicia had recently undergone some kind of makeover—a redo that made Felicia look totally hot. Hot in a way that suggested this girl was going after some serious male attention.

Cassidy didn't get it. After all, Felicia had always been exceptionally pretty—Emma often compared her to Penelope Cruz—and in Cassidy's opinion Felicia did not need to wear sexy clothes or flashy hair and bold makeup to turn a guy's head. They were already looking.

This fact had been driven home in Cassidy's Algebra II class just this morning. Poor Marcus Zimmerman couldn't take his eyes off Felicia as he walked into the classroom, so much so that he didn't notice a stray chair in the aisle and wound up toppling right over it, causing the class to roar with laughter. Naturally, Marcus made a quick recovery, feigning a dramatic bow as if he'd purposely choreographed the whole thing for their entertainment.

Cassidy felt certain his accident was a result of Felicia's short-short skirt and low-cut top. She suspected it was just a matter of time before Felicia was called down to the dean's office and reminded of the school's rigid dress code. Northwood Academy had put an end to the dreaded school uniforms several years back, but as a result the dress code was firmly enforced. At least it used to be.

"We need to talk," Cassidy said quietly to Emma Parks, accosting her friend as she emerged from the restroom and pulling her aside.

Emma's blue eyes grew wide. "What? Are you breaking up with me?" she said in a teasing tone.

"Very funny." Cassidy lowered her voice. "So, did you talk to Felicia yet?"

"No, but I asked her to meet me in the cafeteria to—"

"Well, hold your horses."

"What?"

"I've changed my mind."

"Huh?" Emma's brow creased in confusion. "What d'ya mean?"

"I know we all voted to let Felicia into the DG last week," Cassidy began quietly, "but I—"

"I already told Felicia to meet me at lunch today." Emma pushed a strand of wavy blonde hair behind an ear.

"You need to cool your jets." Cassidy tugged Emma away from what looked like overly interested ears.

"But Felicia is really hoping she's in," Emma persisted. "We need her in order to have an even number of girls for our whole double date—"

"Maybe so. But I am rescinding my vote."

"Rescinding?" Emma frowned. "Meaning you're backing down completely? You don't want Felicia in the DG at all? *Ever?*"

"That's right." Cassidy glanced around to be sure no one could overhear her. "I have reasons to believe Felicia isn't a good fit for the DG."

"What kind of reasons?"

"I'll tell the DG at lunch," Cassidy said. "I just wanted to be sure you hadn't given Felicia the green light yet."

Emma looked skeptical. "You haven't been listening to gossip, have you, Cass? That is so unlike you. But if you have, you better—"

"Hear me out at lunch, okay? I have to get to class now." As Cassidy scurried away, she felt slightly guilty. Was she overreacting? What if the things she'd heard were wrong? But just as she thought this, she saw Felicia hurrying toward the English department. That little yellow skirt was so short that Cassidy felt certain Felicia would be unable to pick a pencil from the floor without exposing her rear end. Why in the world did Felicia think she needed to dress like that anyway? And why in the world hadn't the dean of girls called Felicia into her office by now? What was this school coming to?

• • ● • •

Despite her earlier concerns, Cassidy started doubting herself by the time lunch arrived. Was she being too hasty about Felicia? Too judgmental? Gossipy even? As she entered the cafeteria, she knew that she didn't want to be like that. She despised gossip and was usually outspoken about those who indulged in that kind of meanness. But at the same time, she felt strangely protective of the DG. She didn't miss the irony here since she, of all the girls, had been the most skeptical about a dating club in the beginning.

But after all they'd been through and the friendships the five girls had formed, she felt compelled to preserve the integrity of the DG. To that end, she set her brown bag lunch aside and pulled out her iPad, opening up the rules that they'd written in September. She was just perusing the document when the other girls started trickling up to their usual table.

Dating Game Club Rules

1. We will honor the secret membership of the DG.
2. We will be loyal to our fellow DG members.
3. We will help fellow DG members to find dates with good guys.
4. We will report back to the DG regarding our dates.
5. We will not be jealous over a fellow DG member's boyfriend.
6. We will never steal a fellow DG member's boyfriend.
7. We will abstain from sex on our DG dates.
8. We will not lie to the DG about what happens on our dates.
9. We will never let a boyfriend come between DG members.
10. We will admit new DG members only by unanimous vote.

"Oh no," Bryn said in a teasing tone. "Cass is reading the DG rules again. Time for another little lecture?"

"I don't lecture anyone," Cassidy retorted.

Emma set her tray down with a clunk and a frown. "Cass doesn't want Felicia in the DG," she chanted like a tattletale.

"I guess I'm just having second thoughts," Cassidy clarified. "I rescinded my vote to buy us some time. We need to go over some things before we commit to another member."

"But we already voted." Bryn set her chef salad on the table, tossing her mane of long, sleek blonde hair over her shoulders as she primly took a seat. "Remember?"

"Yes, but Emma hasn't *told* Felicia yet. I'm calling an emergency meeting before she does," Cassidy informed them. "Any objections?"

"Not if you think it's really necessary." Bryn opened a packet of salad dressing.

"I do," Cassidy declared. "Think about it. Does anyone here want to induct a member that we'll regret later on?"

"Good point." Abby focused on unwrapping her bean burrito. "I'd hate to have to kick someone out."

"I have some questions about Felicia," Cassidy said quietly.

"I do too." Devon nodded eagerly as she opened a packet of ketchup.

"Really?" This was totally unexpected, but Cassidy tried to take it in stride. "Yeah . . . okay then. It's obvious we need to discuss this."

"Come on, you guys. What has poor Felicia done to deserve this kind of scrutiny?" Emma demanded. She pointed a finger at Cassidy. "Just so you know, I probably sounded like a stuck-up snob when I told her I couldn't talk right now. Even though I was the one who asked her to meet with me. I could tell by her expression that she thinks I'm just jerking her chain, and I don't blame her a bit. She probably won't even want to join now."

"So what's going on exactly?" Abby narrowed her dark brown eyes at Cassidy. "Why should we have second thoughts about Felicia?"

"I have some concerns," Cassidy stated carefully. "It's partly about her appearance and part—"

"I know what this is," Bryn taunted. "Cassidy and Devon are worried that Felicia's too much competition."

"That's laughable." Devon held her chin high as if to assure everyone that she had no concerns. And why should she? With her wavy auburn hair and curvy figure, she had no problem catching a male eye.

"And totally bogus." Cassidy held up her iPad like it held evidence. "Here's the deal. I don't think Felicia will want to comply with our rules."

"Which rules?" Abby asked with interest.

Cassidy scanned down the rules, stopping her finger on rule #7. "This one for starters." She looked around uneasily. "I'm not sure we should be having this meeting right now . . . in public. Especially not here in the cafeteria."

Emma leaned over, quietly reading the seventh rule loud enough for the others to hear. "We will abstain from sex on our DG dates." Her brow creased as she peered at Cassidy. "What are you saying about Felicia?"

"I'm saying I have reason for concern."

"Did Felicia tell you something that suggests that she can't comply with this rule?" Abby asked pointedly.

"No. But I overheard some girls in choir last week. They were talking about Felicia and—"

"This is about gossip?" Abby's dark brown eyes grew wide. "You of all people, Cass? You hate gossip."

"I know." Cassidy nodded contritely. "I do hate gossip, but it's not just that. I've noticed some things about Felicia—the way she's dressing and acting lately. Something has changed. Trust me, something's not right with that girl."

"I know exactly what Cassidy means," Devon declared. "Felicia is dressing just like a hooker."

"Really, Devon." Emma used a scolding tone. "You should talk."

Devon pursed her lips with angry eyes. "What are you insinuating?"

"Well . . . you *used* to dress like a hooker. Before we made you—"

"I cannot believe you'd say something like—"

"You know it's true. I still have some photos on my phone—"

"And I thought you were my friend!"

"Stop fighting." Cassidy held up a hand. "This is not why I brought this up right now."

"Are you trying to turn lunch into an official meeting?" Abby demanded. "Because I, for one, cannot do this. As soon as I finish eating, I need to get down to the gym to pick up my basketball uniform and get some—"

"This is the wrong place to talk about something like this," Bryn said. "If we need a real meeting, let's go to Costello's like we usually do."

"I agree," Devon said. "I move that we end this meeting."

"It's *not* a meeting," Cassidy pointed out.

"Whatever." Bryn tipped her head to a group of girls standing nearby who were looking at them curiously. "There are too many ears in here. Let's put a lid on it."

"What am I supposed to tell Felicia?" Emma asked.

"Tell her to *wait*," Cassidy urged. "Just until we can meet and get this thing settled."

"Can everyone make it at 5:00?" Bryn asked.

"I might be late," Abby said with her mouth full. "We're starting practice this week. We don't usually quit until 5:00."

"How about 5:30 then?" Cassidy suggested. "It can be a quick meeting."

"You really think we need this?" Bryn demanded.

"I don't," Emma told her.

"I do," Devon shot back at her. "Cassidy is absolutely right. I didn't want to say anything, but I have some questions about Felicia too. I've heard stuff like what Cassie is saying. We need to know what we're getting into . . . before we get into it."

"Well, that's very interesting, considering . . ." Bryn studied Devon with slightly narrowed eyes. "Hmm."

Cassidy knew what Bryn was insinuating. She thought it was a little weird that Devon was speaking out against someone else's character like this. Especially since Devon had come so close to being thrown out of the DG just a few days ago. Although Cassidy appreciated the moral support in her quest to protect the DG, it wasn't too comforting that it only seemed to be coming from Devon. Siding with Devon on something like this was a bit disturbing.

Abby wadded up her napkin. "Okay then, I'll do my best to get to this meeting by 5:30. But you better make it worth my time. I do trust you, Cass. You're a fair person. I know you wouldn't dis on Felicia just because of stupid gossip."

"Or even just because of how Felicia dresses," Bryn added. "Because, as you guys know, we all needed some wardrobe assistance when we started the club." She tipped her head toward Cassidy. "You in particular, girlfriend, were not exactly what I'd call fashion forward, if you recall."

The others laughed and Cassidy felt her cheeks grow warm as she started doubting herself again. Maybe she was wrong about Felicia. "Okay," she said quietly. "I'll try to gather as much information as I can before we meet." However, she had no idea how she was going to do this. What information?

"And I'll help," Devon promised.

"Great." Bryn's blue eyes twinkled with mischief. "I can't wait to hear what you girls dig up on poor Felicia. Sounds juicy."

"Bryn!" Emma glared at her. "I thought you *liked* Felicia." She looked from face to face with a disappointed scowl. "I thought you all liked her."

"I used to like her well enough," Cassidy admitted. "But I don't feel like I really know her anymore. It seems like she's changed."

"Well, I never knew Felicia before this year, but she doesn't seem like the kind of girl the DG needs." Devon sighed. "I know I don't say this much, but I actually like how you guys kinda raised the bar on this whole dating thing. I know I don't always act like it, but I appreciate that you have standards and morals. As you obviously know, I kinda need that in my life."

"I care about the DG." Abby stood up and reached for her bag. "As you all know, my dad's not real thrilled with me dating in the first place. The DG's my only hope. But not if it turns into something skanky. My dad would put the kibosh on that."

"That's true." Bryn nodded. "He would. I guess we need to remember we've created something pretty special here. We need to be careful to keep it that way." She smiled at Cassidy. "Thanks for making us slow down and really consider this."

"I gotta go," Abby said. "See you guys at 5:30."

Emma seemed to soften as Abby left. "Yeah, maybe you're right, Cass," she said quietly. "We don't want to do something we'll regret. As hard as it might be to pass on Felicia, it would be even harder to have to kick her out later on down the line."

"It could ruin the DG for everyone," Bryn said.

"Cass and I will get this figured out," Devon assured them. "We'll bring the facts to everyone at 5:30."

"I'll just tell Felicia to hang . . . and that I'll talk to her later." Emma's mouth twisted to one side. "I do hope you're wrong about her, Cass. I really hope Felicia can be part of the DG. I think she needs us."

Cassidy nodded as she bit into her apple. She didn't want to admit it, but she was feeling uneasy and wondering if Emma might be right. Devon's talk about going out to gather "facts" didn't make her feel any better. How were they supposed to get facts when so far all Cassidy really had was a strong impression combined with what truly was only gossip? To pass judgment on Felicia based on such flimsy evidence . . . how fair was that?

As a child, Devon had always loved playing detective games and reading mysteries. After she outgrew those things, she moved on to crime and police TV series and films. Sometimes she even fantasized about becoming some kind of a sleuth herself—although she'd probably have to get a lot more serious about academics to do so.

However, as she walked toward the gym, Devon felt a sense of excitement. Like she was "on a case." The idea of going undercover to find out the dirt on Felicia was appealing on many levels. To be fair, it wasn't as if she was out to smear the girl's name. She just wanted to get to the bottom of it. If Felicia wound up looking bad as a result, well, that was Felicia's problem. At least that's what Devon told herself as she went into the girls' locker room. As luck would have it, Felicia just happened to be in Devon's fifth period conditioning class.

Devon had probably exchanged less than a dozen words with Felicia since Devon had started school here in the fall. It wasn't that Devon didn't like Felicia—more like she hadn't really gone out of her way to get to know her. Today she was ready to make the first move.

"Hey, Felicia," she said in a friendly tone. "Cute outfit."

Felicia looked surprised, then doubtful. "Uh . . . thanks . . . I guess."

"Showing lots of leg there," Devon said lightly as she started to peel off her clothes for PE.

Felicia just shrugged. "So?"

"I can't believe Mrs. Dorman hasn't called you in yet," Amanda Norton said in a slightly snooty tone.

"I know." Tristin Wilson tossed Felicia a disgusted look. "Did you ever stop to think that dressing like that could get Northwood back into those stupid uniforms again?"

"Ugh, I hated those uniforms." Amanda wrinkled her nose as she wiggled out of her jeans.

"If they bring back the detested uniforms, we'll have Felicia to thank," Tristin added.

Felicia glared at Tristin and Amanda as she grabbed up her stuff, toting it down to the other end of the locker room where she continued to dress by herself.

"What's her problem anyway?" Devon said to no one in particular.

"Haven't you heard?" Tristin looked over her shoulder and giggled.

"Heard what?" Devon asked with interest.

"The reason Felicia dresses like that." Tristin looked at Amanda and laughed in a secretive way.

Devon moved closer to the two girls. "Why?"

"I don't know if we should tell you . . ." Tristin glanced at Amanda.

Amanda firmly shook her head no.

"We can trust Devon," Tristin told Amanda. "She's cool."

"Yeah." Devon tried not to sound overly eager. "You can trust me."

"Felicia's been trying to make a little extra money," Tristin whispered.

"What do you mean?" Devon asked.

Tristin gave a knowing nod. "You know what they say, *dress for the job*."

"Tristin." Amanda gave her friend a warning look. "Watch your mouth."

"Seriously?" Devon feigned a laugh as she tried to absorb their insinuation. Were they just messing with her? Or did they really know something? Seeing Miss Campton coming out of her office, Devon lowered her voice. "Are you really saying that Felicia is a—well, *you know*."

"Haven't you seen her ad on MyPlace.com?" Tristin asked.

"*What?*" Devon watched Miss Campton pinning something onto the bulletin board.

"She advertises for guys," Tristin whispered.

"On MyPlace?" Devon couldn't believe it.

"Look and see." Tristin whispered a sleazy sounding name in Devon's ear. "That's what she calls herself on there."

Devon looked at Amanda now. "Is this really true?"

Amanda just shrugged as she pulled on a tank top.

"Look it up." Tristin shoved her feet into her shoes. "It's all there for everyone to see." She grinned. "Go ahead and tell your guy friends. I'm sure she can use the business."

"Tristin!" Amanda frowned with disapproval. "Knock it off."

But Tristin just laughed.

As Devon pulled on her shorts, she glanced over to where Felicia was pulling on a T-shirt with her back toward them. Devon frowned at Felicia's relatively boring white underwear. If Tristin's insinuations were true, Devon would've expected something a little more risqué. Then again, you never could tell.

Throughout class, Devon couldn't stop thinking about the name Tristin had told her. It sounded like the name of an exotic dancer, or maybe something worse. Anyway, she couldn't wait to investigate this further. She would look it up on her iPhone as soon as she could. If it was for real, it would prove that Cassidy was spot-on in her suspicions about Felicia. A girl like that did not belong in the DG. Furthermore, she didn't belong in this school. Devon wasn't exactly an expert on all the school rules, but she knew there was a code of honor here and, if Tristin was telling the truth, Felicia had broken it.

It wasn't until after the last bell of the day rang that Devon could turn on her iPhone. As she walked to her locker, she entered MyPlace and ran a search on the name Tristin had given her. Sure enough, a page popped up—along with some very skanky-looking shots of Felicia. Devon blinked in surprise as she read some of the suggestive stuff written there—was Felicia crazy? This page could get her kicked out of Northwood in a heartbeat. Or maybe that's what she wanted. Devon remembered when she'd first been forced to attend school here, she'd hoped to get kicked out and return to her old public school. Maybe that was Felicia's game.

As Devon turned toward her locker bay, she knew her friends needed to see this ASAP. They would be nuts to invite Felicia to join the DG. She forwarded the link to all of them. Let them decide for themselves what Felicia was truly like. If they still wanted someone like that in the DG, Devon for one would be outraged.

"Hey, Devon," Cassidy called out as she and Emma came over to where Devon was just closing her locker. "Need a ride home?"

"Sure." Devon grinned victoriously. "You guys checked your phones yet?"

"No." Cassidy reached into her bag, extracting a phone. "What's up?"

"You'll see." Devon poked Emma. "Come on, get out your phone."

As Emma was digging out her phone, Devon nudged Cassidy. "Did you have any luck finding out about Felicia?" she asked.

"A little," Cassidy said as she turned on her phone. "Nothing more than just gossip, really."

"I noticed Felicia going into the counseling center right after sixth period," Emma said a bit glumly. "I'm sure it was to see Mrs. Dorman about how she was dressed. But I felt sorry for Felicia. She looked pretty sad."

"What is *this*?" Cassidy held up her phone. "Is this for real?"

"Does it look like it's real?" Devon challenged.

"Yeah . . . but—"

"What is it?" Emma demanded. "My stupid phone is too slow." She leaned over to see Cassidy's phone. "Show me."

Cassidy held her phone out for Emma to see. "No way!" Emma exclaimed.

"That's Felicia," Cassidy said quietly.

"Yeah, but she'd never put that up—"

"Amanda and Tristin said that she's trying to make money," Devon said quietly, watching her friends' faces. Both Cassidy and Emma seemed appropriately shocked.

"No way," Emma said again. "I don't believe it."

"Then why does she dress like that?" Devon demanded.

"I don't know." Emma frowned. "I just can't believe it."

"Maybe Felicia's family is having financial problems," Devon suggested. "Tuition here isn't exactly cheap, you know."

"Even so." Emma stubbornly shook her head. "I'm not buying it."

"I have to agree with Em on this," Cassidy said. "It's too unbelievable. Felicia would be nuts to put this up on the internet."

"Why would she do it?" Emma demanded.

"Don't you guys pay attention to the news?" Devon asked her. "This stuff is happening all over the country."

"Maybe in the school you used to go to. But in Northwood? I don't think so." Cassidy pursed her lips.

"Who else did you send this to?" Emma demanded.

"Just Abby and Bryn," Devon told her.

"You shouldn't have sent it to anyone," Emma said hotly. "That was wrong."

"But it's on MyPlace," Devon argued. "For the whole world to see."

"That's true," Cassidy agreed. "It's not fair to blame Devon for it being out there. Don't shoot the messenger, Em. I'm actually glad she found this." She pointed at Emma. "You're just in denial."

"It's okay, Em." Devon slipped an arm around her shoulders. "I like that you insist on thinking the best of people. At least sometimes you do." She frowned in Emma's face. "Sometimes you think the worst of me, don't you?"

Emma looked slightly contrite. "I'm sorry, Devon. But sometimes you deserve it."

Devon laughed. "Yeah, I guess you're right."

"Well, if you guys want a ride, let's move it," Cassidy told them. "I have a pile of homework I want to get started on before our meeting at Costello's."

"That should be very interesting," Devon said as she looped the handle of her bag over a shoulder. "I can't wait to see what the others think about this new little development."

"What am I going to say to Felicia?" Emma asked glumly as they walked across the parking lot toward Cassidy's car.

"Why not just tell her the truth?" Cassidy suggested. "Maybe she'll rethink some of her, uh, choices."

"Right." Emma let out a loud sigh. "I'm going to walk up to her and say, hey, Felicia, sorry you can't be in our club because we have rules against hookers."

Devon laughed. "You don't have to be *that* honest."

"Poor Felicia," Emma said as they got into Cassidy's car. "I feel sorry for her."

"Why?" Devon demanded as she got into the passenger seat in front. "It's not like anyone forced her into this—well, whatever it is she's into."

"We still don't know this for sure," Emma said meekly from behind.

"We know that she's been dressing pretty strangely lately," Devon reminded her. "We know that you saw her going into the office of the dean of girls. We know she's got those photos and stuff on MyPlace. And I saw her in the locker room. The way she went off by herself . . . well, it was almost like she was ashamed."

"Can't blame her for that," Cassidy said sadly. "I agree with Emma, I feel sorry for her too."

"So do you want her to be part of the DG?" Devon demanded.

"No, of course, not." Cassidy started to back the car.

"How about you, Em?"

"No . . . not if what you say is true. I can still try to be her friend, though, can't I?"

"You really want to be a friend to a girl like that?" Devon asked.

"Well, I've been a friend to you," Emma declared, "and you've made some pretty stupid mistakes, Devon. Don't forget about that."

"I know." Devon slumped down into the seat. "I've already told you guys that I'm sorry. I really am sorry, and I want to do better."

"We know." Cassidy reached over and patted her on the shoulder. "But we don't need more than one project girl in the club."

"What?" Devon sat up straighter. "You're calling me a project girl now?"

Cassidy laughed. "Sorry, I couldn't resist."

"You have to admit that you've put our friendship to the test," Emma said. "Can you blame me for thinking it's just a little ironic that you're being this hard on Felicia?"

"Just because I care about the DG?" Devon turned around to lock eyes with Emma. "You want to see the DG turn into something that—"

"Stop fighting," Cassidy insisted as she pulled up to the stop sign. "You're going to distract my driving."

"Sorry," Emma mumbled.

"Yeah, me too." Devon slumped back down into the seat. Did her friends really see her like that? Like she was a project? Something they always had to save and rescue? Maybe it was true.

"Now everyone's going to get quiet?" Cassidy asked. "This is the thanks I get for giving you guys a ride?"

"Sorry . . . I was just thinking," Devon told her.

"You haven't told us what's up with your mom," Cassidy said quietly.

"Yeah," Emma chimed in. "Is she really getting married to what's-his-name?"

"Rodney." Devon didn't like the sound of his name or the taste it left in her mouth. "They want to get married around Christmas."

"Oh?" Cassidy glanced her way. "How do you feel about that?"

"Like my mom's lost her mind."

"What's wrong with the guy?"

"Where do I begin?" Devon groaned. Did she really want to go here? And then again, why not? "For starters, he doesn't even have a job. Plus he's younger than my mom."

"Oh no, does that mean your mom's a cougar?"

"I guess." Devon grimaced. "And he tries to act real cool around me. Like I should think he's all that. The truth is, I can't stand him."

24

"For any special reason?" Emma asked. "Or just in general?"

"He's been married a couple of times already, and he's got a little girl from his first marriage. From what I can see, he pretty much ignores her."

"What a lowlife."

"Tell me about it."

"What's your mom see in him?" Cassidy asked.

Devon just laughed.

"He's good-looking," Emma told her. "At least that's what my mom said. I guess she met him a while back."

"He might be good-looking in our moms' eyes," Devon said, "but I think he's a just a big jerk. I'll bet that even if he and Mom do get married, it won't last more than a year, two at best. The good news is that I should be long gone by the time it unravels." She sighed. "But I still don't like the idea of my mom getting her heart broken . . . again."

"It makes me want to be über-careful about the man I marry," Cassidy said somberly. "Not that I'm planning anything. Not until I'm at least thirty anyway." She made a nervous laugh.

Now they all took turns making jokes about guys and marriage, but as Cassidy's car pulled up to Devon's house, Devon felt a dark cloud of sadness settle over her. It was the same black cloud she'd been experiencing ever since her mom had gotten involved with Rodney a few weeks ago. Just the same, she made a stiff smile as she told her friends good-bye. As she got out of the car, giving what she hoped looked like a lighthearted wave, she wished that she had someplace else to go home to. Some other life . . . something different than this.

E mma felt a stab of guilt as she watched Devon going into her house. "I know she's not happy," she said glumly. "But I don't know what to do about it."

"Just keep being her friend," Cassidy said as she drove away.

"Devon isn't the easiest person to be a friend to sometimes." Emma had known Devon for as long as she could remember, and sometimes it felt like they were destined for a never-ending love-hate relationship.

"I know what you mean. But I've kind of incorporated a Scripture into my life recently. Maybe I'll call it my Devon verse."

"What is it? 'Love your enemies'?"

Cassidy laughed. "Devon isn't my enemy."

"I know." Emma felt more guilt. "She's not mine either, but sometimes she makes me kinda crazy—hey, where are you going?" she asked as she realized Cassidy had turned on the wrong street.

"Taking you home?"

"No, remember I said I'm supposed to go to my grandma's today."

"Oh yeah." Cassidy nodded. "I forgot."

"Mom's worried that she's depressed . . . missing my grandpa, ya know. I'm supposed to cheer her up."

Cassidy did a U-turn on the quiet street. "That's nice you can do that, Em."

"So, tell me—what's your magic verse?"

"Well, it's not magic. It's in Second Corinthians. I think it's in chapter twelve. But don't expect me to quote it to you."

"Whatever. Just give me the gist, okay?"

"It's about how God's grace is big enough to help us through anything. When we're at our weakest place—like how hard it is to be a good friend to Devon sometimes—God can step in and become our strength. We just need to realize we're weak and ask him to help us. Anyway, it's something like that. I read it in a devotional book last week and it kinda stuck, ya know?"

"That's pretty cool. Can you text the reference to me so I can look it up too?"

"Sure."

"Maybe it's working for you, Cass. Because it seemed like you and Devon were getting along pretty good today. Better than usual, anyway." Emma frowned. "Of course, it also seemed like you were ganging up against poor Felicia."

"You still think that? After what you saw and heard about her? You think we're ganging up on her just because we want to maintain the integrity of the DG?"

"Yeah, well, when you put it like that, I guess not. But I still feel sorry for her."

"I feel sorry for her too. It looks like she's making some really stupid choices." Cassidy pulled into Emma's grandma's driveway then turned to peer at Emma. "Think about it, we already have one problem child in the DG. You really think we should take on another?"

Emma bit her lip as she gathered her bag. "I don't know . . . maybe not."

"Want a ride to Costello's later?"

"Sure." Emma thanked her for the ride as she opened the door, and as she walked up to the house, she thought about what Cass had said about God's grace being big enough.

"There's my girl." Grandma opened the door and happily hugged Emma. "I've been looking forward to this all day." She led Emma to the kitchen. "I decided that we'd make pumpkin bread. How does that sound to you?"

"Yummy." Emma dropped her bag on a chair and took off her jacket.

"We'll make enough to freeze for Thanksgiving and for you to have some to take home." She opened the oven door. "I already baked the pumpkin and it's nice and cool now. You can do the scraping."

Emma was relieved that Grandma seemed to be in good spirits, but she was still thinking about Devon as she scraped the pumpkin meat into a bowl.

"Is something troubling you?" Grandma asked.

Emma told Grandma about Devon's situation. Oh, she didn't go into all the details—like how Devon had nearly poisoned herself with too much alcohol last weekend—but she did tell her about how Devon's mom was acting pretty irresponsible. "This Rodney dude is a lot younger, and according to Devon, he's a total jerk. She thinks they'll get married in December, and I can tell from how she talks, he's been spending the night at their house sometimes." Emma tossed a big chunk of pumpkin in the bowl. "I can't imagine how upset I'd be if Mom did that to me."

"No, I can't either. But I can't imagine your mother doing something like that in the first place."

"No . . . she wouldn't."

"That's too bad for Devon. I really thought Lisa had better

sense. But she went through that hard divorce. I'm sure that took a toll on her self-esteem. I'll bet that's part of her problem now. Still, it's not fair to Devon." Grandma shook her head as she chopped nuts. "Having a mom's boyfriend spending the night in their home . . . well, that's just wrong. Especially with a teenage girl in the house." She put down her knife with a clank. "And I'm pretty sure Dr. Phil would agree with me on that."

Emma couldn't help but laugh. Grandma was a die-hard Dr. Phil fan. She had all his books and never missed a show—even if it was a rerun. "So I've been wondering . . ." Emma put the last of the pumpkin into the bowl. "Maybe I should offer to let Devon live with us. I'm sure Mom wouldn't mind. Sometimes she gets along better with Devon than she does with me." Emma frowned.

"Oh, honey, that's so sweet that you're willing to share your home with Devon, but do you really think that's a good idea? I know you girls have been close off and on over the years, but I also know you can fight like cats and dogs sometimes too."

"That's true."

Grandma measured some flour, dumping it into the mixing bowl. "I hate to see you feeling like the odd man out—or odd girl out—in your own home. Especially with the holidays coming, when Edward will be home from college. It might be awkward for him having Devon as part of the household."

Emma hadn't even thought about how her brother might react to Devon living with them, but she was actually relieved that Grandma's thinking was taking this route. Because as much as she wanted to help Devon, the idea of having her full-time in their home until graduation was a little scary. "Yeah, those are good points," she admitted. "I hadn't even considered those things."

Grandma paused from measuring salt. "I have an idea, Emma. Something that might be good for both you and Devon—and for me too."

"What?"

"How about if Devon moves in with me?"

"Seriously?" Emma blinked.

"Absolutely. Devon and I have always gotten along well. I know the girl's got a bit of the devil in her—she always has. But thanks to Dr. Phil I've picked up some skills over the years. I think I might be of some use." Grandma smiled.

"Really?" Suddenly Emma felt unsure. Was she truly willing to share her grandma with Devon?

"You know, Emma, it might even be an answer to prayer for me." She sighed. "I've been out of sorts since your grandfather died. I've felt rather lost. Oh, I try to act like I'm fine, but the truth is, I'm lonely."

Emma nodded. "Yeah . . . I know."

"Devon is a little chatterbox."

"That's true."

"And she doesn't have a grandma nearby."

"That's true too."

"And she's almost like family. I've known her mother since she and your mom were in school together." Grandma clasped her hands. "Oh, Emma, this is so exciting. Do you think Devon will be interested?"

"I, uh, I don't know."

"Do you think Lisa will mind?" Grandma pursed her lips. "Although, considering what you've said about this Rodney fellow, I would think Lisa would be relieved."

"Yeah, and then Lisa can do whatever she wants. Have her boyfriend over or disappear for a few days." Emma scowled with disapproval.

"It might even be a wake-up call for Lisa," Grandma said as she measured cinnamon.

"How so?"

"If she sees that choosing to be involved with Rodney like

30

that means that Devon has to live elsewhere . . . well, perhaps she'll rethink the whole business."

"Wouldn't that be nice," Emma said dourly.

"So what's our next step?" Grandma asked hopefully. "Do I call Devon? Or should you?"

Emma frowned with uncertainty. "I'm not sure."

Grandma's mouth twisted to one side as she unwrapped a cube of butter. "Maybe you should call her, Emma. That way, if she's not interested, it won't make her uncomfortable. I wouldn't want to pressure her at all. Of course, she would have to understand that she would be subject to some house rules if she comes here. I certainly wouldn't want her to think she could just run wild."

"No . . . that wouldn't be good." Emma felt even more uncertain now. What if Devon accepted this offer, thinking it was her ticket to complete freedom?

It wasn't long until all the ingredients were mixed and the bread pans were filled with spicy-smelling batter. As Grandma closed the oven door, she turned hopefully to Emma. "Why don't you call Devon right now, honey? I'm dying to hear her answer. Even if it is no."

"Okay . . ." Emma reluctantly went to get her phone, remaining in the living room as she hit the speed dial. What if this was all a big mistake?

"Hey, Em," Devon said in a slightly flat-sounding voice. "What's up?"

"Well, I have kind of a crazy idea—actually my grandma has a crazy idea." Slowly, Emma explained. The other end of the line was so silent that Emma wondered if she'd lost the connection. "Devon?" she said. "Are you still there?"

"Yeah . . . I'm here." Devon's voice sounded even stranger now.

"Are you okay?" Emma asked nervously. "You haven't been getting into your mom's booze again, have you?"

"No, of course not. I told you I was never doing that again."

"Yeah, but you say lots of things."

"Are you calling me a liar?"

"No—I'm sorry. It's just that I care about you."

"Yeah . . . sorry . . . I know."

"So, what do you think? Or maybe you need time to think about it. Or to talk to your mom . . . or whatever. I just promised Grandma I'd call and let you know."

"I can't believe this."

"What?"

"That your grandma would really ask me something like this."

"Huh?" Emma was confused. Was Devon insulted by her grandma's offer? If she was, shouldn't Emma be insulted that Devon would react like that? After all, Grandma was doing this out of the goodness of her heart. "What do you mean—ask you something like this? Are you saying—"

"I'm just kinda blown away, that's all."

"Oh?"

"You know what I was just doing?" Devon asked in a serious voice.

"I have no idea."

"I was on my knees, Emma."

"Huh?"

"I was *praying*."

"Seriously?"

"Yeah. I can hardly believe it myself. But I felt so desperate when I came into the house. I literally got down on my knees and I begged God to get me out of this place. I hate being here, Emma. I despise it. I mean, it used to be okay, but now that Rodney's acting like he's part of the family, it's unbearable. When I walked into the house and saw his leather motorcycle jacket hanging by the front door, I almost went ballistic. It feels like he's marking his territory—you know, how a dog does in a yard. Anyway, I was seriously tempted to stuff that stupid jacket into the fireplace, douse it with something flammable and just light it on fire."

"But you didn't?"

"No. I knew that would just make more problems."

"For sure. But you were actually praying?"

"I was."

"Wow." Emma glanced over to the kitchen where Grandma was cleaning up the baking tools. "So what do you think then?"

"I think—yes, yes, yes!" Devon said happily. "Ask your grandma how soon I can move in."

"Don't you need to talk to your mom?"

"Did she talk to me before bringing Rodney into our lives?"

"I guess not."

"Seriously, Em, ask your grandma when I can come, okay? I'll start packing right now."

Emma went into the kitchen now. "Grandma?"

Grandma looked up from where she was setting a bowl in the dishwasher. "Yes?"

"Devon wants to know when she can come."

Grandma's eyes lit up and she laughed. "Whenever she likes."

"Did you hear that?" Emma said into the phone. "Grandma said whenever."

"Cool. Maybe I'll pack a bag and walk over there right now," Devon said. "Is that okay?"

"Can Devon come right now?" Emma asked her grandma.

"Tell Devon that the pumpkin bread will be out of the oven in about thirty minutes." Grandma grinned as Emma relayed this message and hung up. "Well, isn't that amazing," Grandma said happily.

"Do you want to hear what's really amazing?" Emma asked. "Devon told me that she was actually praying just now, asking God to give her another place to live."

Grandma's eyes got misty. "Well, isn't that just how God works sometimes—miraculously." She dried her hands on a towel. "Want to help me clear some things out of the spare bedroom to make more room for Devon?"

"Sure," Emma said without real enthusiasm. Oh, she was happy for Devon and even happier for Grandma. But a juvenile and selfish part of her was feeling pea green with jealousy too. What if Devon tried to take Emma's place with her grandmother?

I t was only the first week of November, but as Bryn pointed out at the student council meeting after school, it was not too soon to be working on the Christmas ball. "In fact," she declared hotly, "I think we should've started on it weeks ago." She pointed a manicured finger at Jason Levine. "As president, you should know better than put it off this long."

"Wow," he said smoothly. "You feel pretty strongly about this, don't you?"

She waved a paper in the air. "You didn't even put it on today's agenda, Jason. Never mind that you have no committee—I'll bet you haven't even reserved a location yet."

"Why reserve a location for an outdated event that only a handful of people will attend anyway?"

"That's so not true," Bryn declared. "Lots of us look forward to the Christmas ball."

"It's the least attended event at Northwood," he said with nonchalance. "I already had a conversation with the administration about canceling it this year."

"You want to cancel the Christmas ball?" she demanded.

"I didn't say I *wanted* to cancel it. I said we discussed it, that's all."

"Well, the Christmas ball is a tradition at Northwood. We're one of the few schools that even have a *Christmas* ball. Everyone else calls theirs a *Winter* ball. Like they're afraid of the word *Christmas*! And I for one am not going to take this sitting down, Jason Levine. I will not let the Christmas ball go without a fight." She shook her fist in the air for emphasis.

He smiled as if amused. "Wow, Bryn, why don't you tell us how you really feel?"

Some male members of the council just laughed, but she turned to the crowd with a passionate plea. "Okay, so maybe you guys aren't into this dance—as usual. But how about you girls? Are you ready to kiss the Christmas ball good-bye? To give up a time-honored tradition just because Jason Levine thinks it's outdated? Really?"

Several of the girls, who outnumbered the boys by about two to one, shouted out their support for the dance. Bryn turned back to Jason. "Should we put this to a vote?"

He shrugged. "Nah. I get your point."

"So we need to jump on this," she told him. "Do you know how hard it can be to book a decent ballroom in December? Everyone is having Christmas parties. Remember?"

"Fine. We'll save ourselves some money and hold the ball in the gym."

"In the gym?" she shot back. "Seriously?" She turned to look at the other council members again. "How many of you girls want to go to the Christmas ball in a gym that reeks of smelly basketball players?" The girls made disgusted faces.

"We can fumigate," Jason said. "Knowing how you girls drench yourselves in perfume, it probably won't even be necessary." Naturally this brought out the chuckles from the few guys present.

As Bryn turned back to Jason, she tried to remember why she'd ever found him attractive before. The guy was a jerk. She grimly shook her head. "You may go down in Northwood history, Jason Levine, as the worst student council president of all time."

"Why, thank you, Bryn. Thank you very much." He stood and made a phony bow, then checked his watch. "Now that we've heard Bryn's complaints, does anyone else have anything to add to today's meeting or should we close this—"

"I want to nominate Bryn Jacobs as chairman of the Christmas ball," a girl called out.

"I second the nomination," another yelled.

"All in favor?" Jason asked before Bryn could object. Everyone yelled "yea," and now Jason turned to Bryn. "There you go, Bryn. If the Christmas ball is a flop, you'll only have yourself to blame."

"But I—"

"Thanks for coming, everyone," he called out. "Meeting dismissed."

"Wait, everyone," Bryn yelled as the chairs screeched and people stood. "Before you guys leave, I'm going to put a sign-up sheet by the door. Anyone interested in helping with the Christmas ball, please, talk to me. We can make this an unforgettable night—for everyone." She hurried to the door, planting herself beside it with an open notebook and a pen in hand.

"Come on," she coaxed as people walked past her without signing up. "It will be fun, and it will look good on your college applications. I promise I'll bring food to planning meetings."

Lane Granger lingered, looking curiously at her. "Okay," he said a bit reluctantly as he reached for the pen. "I need more volunteer projects in my college bio."

"Thanks, Lane." She grinned. "It'll be fun. I promise."

Amanda Norton paused by the door as if considering.

"Come on, Amanda." Bryn pushed the pen toward her. "You were on the committee last year, weren't you?"

"Yeah."

"I bet you've got some great ideas." Bryn smiled brightly. "I'd love to have you as my co-chairwoman."

Amanda's mouth twisted to one side as if weighing this invitation.

"Co-chair for a big event like this would look good on college applications," Bryn pointed out.

"I wasn't even planning on *going* to the dance," Amanda said dourly.

"Why not?" Bryn asked. "I realize your boyfriend is in college, but won't he be home for Christmas break? Wouldn't it be fun to get dressed up and go to the Christmas ball with him? And to know that you helped to make it the wonderful night that it will be?"

"Who says I'm even still going with that guy?" Amanda flicked her eyes toward the ceiling then reached for the pen. "Whatever."

"Thank you so much!"

Amanda handed the pen back. "I'll have to coerce Tristin into helping too. And maybe Sienna Abernathy." She pointed at Bryn. "You better get some of your girlfriends to sign up too. The more workers we have, the less work there will be for us."

Bryn beamed at her. "See, already you're acting like a good co-chair. Thanks, Amanda."

"Yeah, I hope I'm not sorry." Amanda glared over to where Jason was still up front, gathering up some papers. "I almost quit student council," she said quietly, "after I heard Jason got elected president. What a farce. Like he really cares about student government. He just thinks this will look good on his college application."

Bryn shrugged. "He's just a figurehead," she whispered. "No one really listens to him anyway."

Amanda snickered. "Let's keep it that way."

Bryn managed to coerce a couple more volunteers to sign up and was just getting ready to leave when Jason came over to look at her sign-up sheet. "Not bad, Bryn. Looks like we got the right person to chair this gig. Thanks for stepping up."

"Thanks to your lack of leadership," she said as she shoved the sign-up sheet into her bag.

He leaned forward to peer closely at her face. "Why do you hate me?"

"Hate you?" She shrugged. "I'm sorry to disappoint you, Jason, but I've never given you enough thought to actually hate you."

He shook his head with narrowed eyes. "That's not true and you know it. You really tore into me up there today. Everyone could see it. And that makes me curious."

"About what?" She pushed a long strand of blonde hair behind an ear as she stepped away from him like he was poison. She hadn't forgotten how he'd treated Devon after the homecoming dance. Bryn wouldn't touch this jerk with a ten-foot pole.

"Usually when a girl pushes as hard as you did, she's secretly trying to send a guy a signal." He smiled. "Like she's really interested and just wants to cover it up."

Bryn laughed. "You're totally delusional, Jason. You're about as interesting to me as a bad case of head lice."

Jason looked offended. "That's not very nice."

"You're right," she admitted. "But it's what you deserve."

"What do you mean?" He looked truly perplexed now.

She narrowed her eyes. "I know what happened with you and Devon after homecoming. It disgusted me."

He tipped his head to one side. "What exactly did she tell you?"

Bryn tried hard to remember. The truth was, Devon hadn't told them a lot. She'd clearly been upset and crying, and her clothes were messed up as if there'd been a tussle at the very least. All in all, it had seemed a pretty bad scene. One that Bryn didn't care to see replayed—with anyone. "Thankfully, I don't recall all the gory details, Jason. But it made you look like a total lowlife. One thing I do remember though—I wanted to call the police."

"Are you kidding?" He looked shocked.

"Not in the least. But Devon wouldn't let us."

"Well, did Devon tell you about anything she'd done? Did she describe how she'd led me on?"

Bryn just shrugged, trying to act nonchalant, uninterested.

"Did Devon tell you how she got me to go out with her?"

"What do you mean?"

"Don't you remember how Devon was doing your bidding, Bryn? She was supposed to get me to go out with you." He made a slightly hangdog look. "That would've been so much better. Trust me. Devon was a huge mistake. I should've known better."

"Yeah. Right." She folded her arms in front of her. She was so not going to be reeled in by this jerk.

"Instead of setting me up with you, like she was supposed to do, Devon enticed me to take her out. Remember?"

"That's not exactly the version I heard," Bryn argued.

"Sure. Why would Devon tell you that she was making the move on your man?"

"My man?" Bryn glared at him. "Ha!"

He laughed. "Okay, that was an overstatement, but I know the games you girls are playing in your little club."

"What games? What little club?" She feigned an oblivious look.

"Okay, maybe I don't know everything, Bryn Jacobs, but I do know you girls have been up to something—since the beginning of the school year."

"That's right," she said sharply. "We've been up to being friends. You got a problem with that?"

He held up his hands defensively. "No problem. I just have a problem with being on your most-hated list. I don't think I deserve that."

She considered this. "Fine. I'll take you off my most-hated list." She moved toward the door. "Satisfied?"

"Better than nothing. But it would be nice if you could give a guy a second chance. I mean, we're in student council together. Might be nice if we could be friends. Who knows, I might want to help with the Christmas ball."

"Yeah, right."

"If it would help us to be friends, Bryn, I would."

She pulled out the sign-up sheet and thrust it at him. "Fine. Consider yourself officially on the committee."

He wrote down his name and phone number and handed it back. "Thanks for giving me a second chance."

She shoved the paper back into her bag. "I guess everyone deserves a second chance, Jason. Hopefully you won't blow it."

A smile lit up his face, and there was no denying the boy was good-looking. With his short black hair and electric blue eyes, he was strikingly handsome. Still, Bryn knew enough about him to know she needed to be careful.

"I hope I can prove to you that I'm not the guy you think I am."

"Time will tell," she said lightly, heading for the door.

"Maybe you can help to rehabilitate me," he said in a teasing tone as he followed her out. "I have a feeling that a girl like you can bring out the best in a guy."

She shook her head with narrowed eyes. "You, Jason Levine, are a cad."

"A cad? Seriously, you're calling me a cad?" He laughed as he walked with her. "What's a cad?"

Now she laughed. "That's a guy who'll say anything to win a girl's trust—when he is clearly not trustworthy."

Jason looked so crushed that Bryn felt a bit guilty. "Okay, that was a bit harsh," she admitted. "But be warned, I'll be keeping my guard up around you, Jason."

He just nodded. "Okay. I get that."

Despite her strong words, Bryn knew that she was softening up toward him. Oh, not soft enough to be anything beyond a cautious friend. But as he walked her down toward the PE department, chatting amicably all the way, she knew that she needed to be careful. Jason had the kind of charm that could wear a girl down, and she had no intention of getting involved with him.

"What are you doing in the girls' gym?" he asked as she paused by the door. "You're not a jock."

She made a face. "Not that it's any of your business, but I'm waiting for Abby to finish practice so I can give her a ride."

He nodded. "Oh yeah. That's right. I better get going. I already missed most of practice myself."

As Bryn went into the girls' gym, she tried to figure Jason out. Why was he being so nice to her? Was he really the kind of person she'd assumed he was? She wondered about what he'd said about Devon. Was it possible that Devon had pulled a fast one on Bryn? Not that Bryn had cared particularly—her initial attraction to Jason had been purely superficial. She knew that he and Amanda were history, and it had seemed like an opportunity at the time.

She'd been a little irked at Devon, but then after that fateful first date when Devon had called the DG in distress, Bryn had simply counted her lucky stars that it hadn't been her. Now she wondered . . . perhaps Jason wouldn't have acted like that with her. Perhaps because Bryn tried to maintain herself as a "lady," he would've treated her as such. It was possible.

She knew Devon well enough to know that girl was as predictable as the November weather. Hadn't she proved it to the DG enough times? Maybe it was unfair to put all the blame of the night onto Jason. After all, there were always two sides to every story. As Bryn took a seat on a bleacher, watching as the girls' team finished up a scrimmage, she decided that the fiasco that had erupted between Devon and Jason a couple months ago could've been the fault of both of them. They were simply a bad combination—like oil and water or, perhaps more fitting, gasoline and matches.

As the basketball girls dribbled and yelled and shot and missed, Bryn opened up the paperback she'd been assigned last week. She was only about a third of the way through *The Grapes of Wrath* but needed to have it finished by Thursday. It was hard to relate to all the trials and tribulations of the poor Joad family, but it was interesting—in a sad, deprived sort of way. It did make her thankful for a relatively comfortable life. Although she had moments when she thought that it might be better to be poor and have a strong sense of family than to be well-off and feel isolated.

• • ● ● •

Basketball practice ended, and before long Bryn and Abby were walking out to the parking lot. Bryn told Abby about the student council meeting and how Jason had nominated her to chair the Christmas ball. "Then he actually offered to be on the committee."

"How can you stand being around him?" Abby asked as she took a swig from her water bottle.

"You know, he might not be as bad as we all thought."

"Seriously?" Abby frowned. "Do you not remember what he did to Devon?"

"I remember Devon being really upset and how she said they'd been in a fight. I don't remember much more than that. Do you?"

Abby took another swig. "I guess not. Just the same, I'd keep a safe distance from that boy."

"Don't worry. I will." Bryn reached in her bag for her phone and pulled up what Devon had sent to them earlier. "Have you looked at your phone lately?"

"No. Should I?"

Bryn handed her phone to Abby. "Devon sent this MyPlace connection to all of us."

"Is that Felicia?" Abby stopped walking to stare down at the phone.

"Seems to be."

"Oh. My. Goodness." Abby shook her head and handed the phone back with a disgusted expression. "I feel like I need to go take another shower now."

"I know. Pretty nasty stuff."

"So Cass was right about her."

"Apparently."

"And Devon too."

"Yeah. Emma was still in denial about it, but it seems pretty clear what we need to do."

"Do we even need a meeting?"

"Probably not. But I've been looking forward to a pumpkin latte all afternoon."

"Sounds good. And maybe we'll need to help Emma see why Felicia is really not DG material."

"Good idea."

"Now we'll have to come up with another girl. I mean, if we're going to go through with the double date thing—and to be honest, I've really been looking forward to it. I'm pretty sure Kent's interested too. He hinted about taking me on a date with just the two of us, but you know what my dad would say about *that*. A double date will be my best bet. We need to get another girl into the club to make it even, though."

As she unlocked her car, Bryn thought about Amanda Norton. She'd been so congenial in agreeing to co-chair the dance. Bryn didn't really know Amanda that well and in the past she'd assumed Amanda was a snob. Maybe she was wrong about her. Just because Amanda was pretty and popular didn't mean she wasn't nice, and unless Bryn had misunderstood, Amanda was single again. She wondered if Amanda might be good DG material. However, she knew that to suggest such a thing would probably get a strong reaction—and not a positive one either. It would take some serious persuasive powers on Bryn's part to get the DG interested in Amanda. Even if the girls bought into this idea, Amanda might just laugh in their faces.

Abby liked to think of herself as a strong person. The kind of girl who didn't need to glom onto a boy just to feel valuable. In the past, she'd sometimes made fun of girls like Devon—occasionally even teased her best friend Bryn—for being "boy crazy." In Abby's opinion, that wasn't simply a personal weakness—it was really lame. Yet, more and more lately she'd found herself thinking about Kent. Wanting to get to know him better. Longing to go out on a "real" date. What was up with that? Furthermore, what kind of hissy fit would her dad throw if he had any idea what was going through his only daughter's mind? He would probably think she was "shallow" and "distracted" and "settling for less" and all sorts of other negative things.

She knew this was partly due to Dad's childhood. Growing up African American in the inner city, where young men got sucked into gangs and drugs, and having a single mom who literally laid down her life to ensure that her son did better, well, Dad maintained some pretty high standards. And Abby understood that.

She'd always been proud of her academic-minded parents. She liked that they both taught college-level classes, that they were actively involved in the community and committed to their church. But sometimes the parental pressure to measure up—to succeed in everything—just got to her. Sometimes the idea of being just a regular girl with a regular boyfriend had a very strong, albeit secret, appeal.

"You're being awfully quiet," Bryn said as she parked the car in front of Costello's. "Everything okay?"

Abby sighed as she reached for her bag. "Just thinking. And maybe I'm a little tired from practice."

"Looked like the coach was working you girls hard," Bryn said as they got out.

"Yeah. She always drives us hard at first."

"You're okay with that?"

"It's just how it is."

"I remember last year, after basketball season ended. You said you weren't going to play this year. You said it was getting way too hard-core competitive. Remember?"

"I know. But it would crush my dad if I quit."

"So you're playing ball to please him?"

Abby shrugged. "Maybe."

"You are such a devoted daughter," Bryn teased. "My father should be so lucky." She laughed.

"I happen to *like* basketball," Abby said stubbornly. And it was true. She did like it—as a recreational sport or shooting hoops in the driveway. But Bryn was right too. The varsity team was getting too competitive to be much fun. It seemed like the girls played rougher and rougher each year. Still, she wasn't ready to confess this to anyone. "Besides that, I don't want to be a quitter," she admitted.

Bryn put her arm around Abby's shoulders. "I know. That's a great quality. But are you sure it's worth it?"

"It would kill my dad if I quit."

"What if it kills you?"

Abby laughed. "That's ridiculous. Besides, it keeps me fit." She poked Bryn's midsection. "Meanwhile, my friend, you are getting a bit flabby."

"I am *not*." Bryn gave Abby a playful shove as they went into Costello's. "And to think I was going to treat you to coffee."

Abby made a face as Bryn stepped up to order their pumpkin lattes. But when it came time to pay, Bryn wouldn't let her. So Abby went over to the other girls, who were already seated at a table.

"Sorry to be late," she told them. "Coach made us run laps at the end of practice."

"Ugh." Devon made a face. "I can't believe you willingly go out for a sport like that, Abby. Are you nuts?"

"Some people think so." Abby glanced up at Bryn as she joined them.

"We need to keep this meeting short and sweet," Cassidy told them. "I have to be home by six."

"Well, you called the meeting," Bryn reminded her. "Go for it."

"Okay." Cassidy laid her iPad on the table. It was open to the MyPlace page with Felicia's provocative photos. "Well, everyone has seen this, right?" She glanced at Abby.

"Yeah." Abby frowned. "Pretty disgusting."

"So, let's put it to a vote. Anyone who still wants Felicia in the DG, raise your hand."

No hands went up, but Emma scowled as if she was unhappy.

"Do you still want Felicia to be in the DG?" Abby asked curiously.

"No . . . ," Emma said slowly. "But I still have a hard time believing she'd do something like this."

"It's right here." Cassidy pointed to the iPad.

"Yeah, but you guys know as well as I do that some MyPlace pages are fakes. Sometimes other people put them up."

"Why would anyone do that?" Bryn demanded.

"To hurt Felicia?" Emma suggested.

"Even so, how would you explain the way Felicia has been dressing?" Cassidy added. "You saw her."

"Bad taste?" Emma shrugged.

"And how about the rumors circulating the school?" Devon asked.

"Mean girls?" Emma said meekly.

"Admit it, Em, whatever is going on with Felicia, it's not good." Cassidy closed the iPad as the barista brought some of the coffees to the table.

"So we all agree then?" Devon asked after the barista left. "Felicia is out of the running?"

Everyone nodded in agreement, quietly sipping their coffees.

"Does that mean we're going to give up on the double-date plan?" Abby asked. "Because I happen to think it's a great idea. I've really been looking forward to it."

"I actually thought we might do it for the Christmas ball," Bryn said.

"Isn't that a long ways off?" Devon complained.

"It's about a month out," Bryn explained.

"Can't we plan something sooner?" Devon begged them. "That's a long time to wait for a date."

"Have you forgotten the mess you made of our last big date?" Emma said sternly. "We all probably need a month to recover."

Devon glared at her.

"I don't mind waiting until the Christmas ball," Abby said. "I'm pretty busy with basketball right now."

"And this gives us time to set up some good dates," Bryn

pointed out. "I, for one, want to go with a guy that I really want to go out with. If you get what I mean."

"It might be cool if we got the guys to ask us out this time," Emma added.

"I agree," Bryn declared, "although that could be a challenge."

"And November is going to be busy enough," Cassidy told them. "Between midterms, the school's fall fund-raiser, and Thanksgiving, December isn't really that far off."

Devon didn't look overly pleased at this plan, but Emma's words seemed to have shut her up.

"Should we write down which guys we want to go with?" Abby asked hopefully. "Just so there's no misunderstanding between girls?"

"Does everyone know?" Cassidy asked.

"I do," Abby declared. "I've got my eye on Kent again."

Cassidy wrote this down.

"And I'd like to go with Isaac again," Emma said a bit shyly. "I mean, if he wants to go with me. I think he might."

"Anyone else have a guy in mind?" Cassidy asked.

"Not really," Bryn told her. "I'm glad I'll have plenty of time to look around."

"I can think of several guys," Devon said, "but I don't want to commit to anything yet."

"I, uh, I might try to see if Lane's interested," Cassidy said with some uncertainty.

"If he's not interested in you, maybe he'll be interested in me." Devon said this with a mischievous glint in her eye.

"Devon," Emma said in a warning tone. "That's not very nice."

Cassidy looked slightly blindsided, but just shrugged. "Well, I guess that's okay," she told Devon. "If Lane's not into me, it's not like I can do anything about it."

"It's still rude," Emma protested. "What about the DG rules? We're not supposed to steal anyone's boyfriend. Remember?"

"Lane is *not* Cassidy's boyfriend," Devon clarified.

"That's true," Cassidy said.

"Even so, Cassidy has stated that she'd like to go to the Christmas ball with him," Bryn interjected. "We need to respect that, Devon."

Devon winked at her. "I was just jerking her chain anyway. I have no intention of going after Lane."

"So, back to the double date thing," Abby said. "There are five of us. Either we do a double date and a triple date or we need to find another DG member."

"I have an idea," Bryn said suddenly.

Everyone looked expectantly at Bryn.

"Who?" Devon asked.

"Amanda Norton," Bryn announced.

"Amanda Norton?" Emma frowned. "She's so stuck up."

"She's really pretty," Devon said.

"She's actually rather nice,' Bryn told them. "She even agreed to help me with the Christmas ball."

"What about her college boyfriend?" Cassidy questioned.

"Apparently they're history," Bryn said.

"But Amanda Norton?" Emma still looked skeptical. "She probably wouldn't even want to be part of the DG."

"Don't be so sure," Bryn said.

"Would she agree to the rules?" Cassidy asked.

"I don't know why not."

"What about her friends?" Cassidy said. "If Amanda joins, Tristin and Sienna might want to join too."

"We don't want them in the DG," Emma declared.

"Why not?" Devon demanded. "I like them. And that would make eight girls in the DG. If you ask me, that would be a lot more fun."

Emma glared at her.

"I don't see anything wrong with the DG growing," Bryn told them. "As long as the girls all agree to the rules."

They discussed and argued about this until Cassidy pointed out the time. "I want to make a motion," she said as she shoved her iPad into her bag. "I move that Bryn should talk to Amanda. She should find out if she's even interested in joining the DG. All in favor, say aye."

They all agreed, but Abby could tell by Bryn's expression that she wasn't satisfied.

"What's wrong?" Abby demanded.

"It's just that it'll be a little awkward, you know? Asking Amanda if she's interested and—so she says yeah and then I just leaving her hanging? How rude is that? I mean, if she's game—and that's probably a long shot—why can't we just invite her to join us?"

They discussed this briefly, finally agreeing that it made sense. Abby made the motion this time, they all voted, and it was unanimous. The meeting was adjourned.

"Oh, one more thing," Bryn said as they were gathering their stuff to leave. "I need you guys to be on the Christmas ball committee. Can I sign you all up?"

"Not me," Abby told her. "I'm too busy with basketball."

Bryn gave Abby a reluctant nod. "Okay, I'll let you off this time. But the rest of you?"

As they were leaving Costello's, Bryn told them all the reasons they should be on the committee, and by the time they got outside, she'd gotten Cass, Em, and Devon signed up.

"You're pretty persuasive," Abby told Bryn as they got back in her car. "Maybe you should go into politics."

Bryn laughed as she started the car. "Maybe I will."

"I wanted to ask if we could specify who we want to go on our double dates with," Abby said as Bryn pulled out.

"I thought you already took care of that," Bryn said in a teasing tone. "We all know you're crushing on Kent, Abs. No competition there."

"That's not what I meant," Abby said a bit tersely. "I meant which other couple."

"Oh." Bryn nodded. "You think we should have that set up too?"

"Maybe." Abby wasn't so sure anymore. At first she'd wanted to double with Bryn, but now she was having doubts.

"You want to double with me and my guy?" Bryn asked hopefully.

"I guess."

"You guess?" Bryn sounded hurt. "What's that supposed to mean?"

"Nothing. Of course, I want to go with you and your date, silly." But even as Abby said this, she was having second thoughts.

Bryn laughed. "Okay then. We'll tell the others tomorrow."

"I'm glad we have plenty of time to get our dates lined up," Abby told her. "I'm not sure how we'll get the guys to do the asking this time. Do you have any ideas?"

"We'll just have to start working on them," Bryn said with confidence. "We'll start dropping lots of clues and—hey—I've just come up with what might be a brilliant plan."

"What is it?"

Bryn's forehead creased as she drove down Main Street. "Okay, it's still kind of congealing in my head. It would be sort of like a campaign to promote the Christmas ball, you know?"

"Not really."

"A way to get the guys all enthused and buying tickets and making plans to go."

"How do you intend to do that?"

"By making it some kind of competition. You know how guys like to compete over everything. So there would be some kind of prize. Maybe we'd get some business to donate it. We'd have posters up all over the school to promote it. That way a girl could point to a poster—you know, while having a conversation with her main crush—and she could sort of challenge him. Does this make any sense?"

"Not really."

"I know." Bryn nodded. "It's pretty half-hatched, I'll admit it. I do think I could be onto something, though."

"Okay." Abby was trying to be a good sport and play along. "Your idea of a prize—what kind of prize would it be? It probably needs to be big in order to get the kind of attention you're talking about. Would it be like a car or a—"

"No way. Who would donate a car?"

"I'm just saying. If you want to get people on board, you have to make it worthwhile."

"I get that, but a car would be impossible."

"Motorcycle?"

"Get real." Bryn laughed. "A skateboard is more likely."

"Right. I can just see those boys jumping through the hoops to get a skateboard, Bryn."

"I know, but how could we possibly get a bigger prize?"

Abby thought hard. "What if the competition was some kind of fund-raiser?"

"November is fund-raising month for the school."

"Yeah." Abby's parents were always involved in some kind of fund-raiser. "But that's just to raise money for Northwood. What if we were raising money for something else? Something more charitable, you know? After all, Christmas is around the corner. What if it was something connected to helping the needy at Christmas? Maybe children in the community."

"Wow, Abs, I like how you think. I feel like we're getting close on this."

They were already at Abby's house. "Let's both keep noodling on it," Abby told Bryn as she got out of the car. "In fact, I'll ask my parents for some suggestions. They might really get into something like this." She waved good-bye and hurried through the raindrops that were starting to pelt down. Getting involved in a fund-raiser might have even more benefits than she'd considered initially. Perhaps she could use working on a fund-raiser as an excuse to cut basketball out of her already busy schedule. It might be worth a shot.

Cassidy had serious misgivings about Bryn's idea of inducting Amanda into the DG, and she planned to make them known at lunchtime the following day. First she had to make sure that Bryn hadn't already invited Amanda.

"I haven't seen her yet," Bryn admitted, "but I just spotted her friends over there. I'm sure she'll be coming in soon."

"Well, I want to raise some questions before it's too late," Cassidy began.

"Oh no, here she goes again," Abby teased. "Cass is going to put the kibosh on every single girl we consider for the DG."

"Yeah, what's up with that?" Bryn demanded. "Amanda would be a great addition. She's pretty and—"

"Looks aren't everything," Cassidy said a bit too quickly.

"Jealous, are we?" Devon taunted.

"No." Cassidy took in a deep breath. "Okay, I know this isn't an official meeting, but you guys need to listen to me. I thought of a number of things that no one mentioned last night."

"For instance?" Devon asked.

"For instance, Amanda is a senior. We're all juniors. What if Amanda joins and tries to pull rank on us? What if she tries to take over?"

"We won't let her," Devon declared.

"How can you be so sure?" Cassidy asked her. "Besides that, Amanda has done a lot of dating. She's had a lot more experience with guys and—"

"That might be a good thing," Bryn pointed out. "She can help us along a little."

"What if she helps us in the wrong sorts of ways?" Cassidy challenged. "Do we really need someone like Amanda to come in and mess things up for us? Is that what you guys want?"

"Wow, you really don't like her, do you?" Bryn said in disbelief. "I thought you were such a good Christian, Cass. Aren't we supposed to love everyone?"

"Yes. I am and I do. I mean, I try to." Cassidy was flustered. "It's not that I don't like Amanda. The truth is, Amanda probably doesn't like me. She's always been kinda uppity and snooty and superior." Cassidy pointed at Emma. "Hasn't she been like that to you too?"

Emma shrugged.

"Tell the truth," Cassidy pressed her.

"In the past . . . not recently . . . Amanda was kind of mean." Emma looked at Cassidy. "To both of us."

"What do you mean 'not recently'?" Bryn asked her.

"It was back in middle school," Cassidy explained. "Amanda Norton was kind of a bully."

"I don't know if I'd call her a bully," Emma clarified. "It's true that she was mean, but it was middle school. Lots of girls were mean."

"Some of them still are," Abby added.

"Not Amanda," Bryn said defensively.

"Maybe she's changed," Devon suggested. "It would be nice to think that people can change, wouldn't it?"

"Yeah." Abby nodded.

Bryn pointed at Cassidy. "You want to talk to Amanda with me? Maybe ask her about some of these things?"

Cassidy cringed. It was the last thing she wanted to do. "Not really."

"The more I think about it, the less I think Amanda will even be interested," Emma proclaimed. "Maybe we should just forget about her."

"Here's something else to consider," Abby said suddenly. "What if Amanda isn't trustworthy? What if she tells everyone about our club? We've been trying to keep it under wraps. If Amanda has a big mouth as well as a mean streak, who knows what she might do."

"Here's what I'll do," Bryn told them. "I'll just kinda test her out. I'll ask some questions and see how she responds. If I have any concerns, I won't even consider asking her. How's that sound?"

They all agreed it sounded like a good plan and Bryn even promised to wait until the first Christmas ball meeting before she broached the subject with Amanda. "That will seem more natural," she assured them.

Everyone else seemed satisfied as they got ready to leave, but Cassidy still had some reservations. Abby had raised a very good point. What if Amanda wasn't trustworthy? What if she blabbed to all her friends about the DG? What if she turned their secret club into a big fat joke?

As Cassidy made her way to class, she stewed over these things. She wondered whether or not she'd care to remain in a club with someone like Amanda Norton in it too. Okay, she knew that sounded pretty judgmental, but those were her honest feelings. As she went into class, she wondered about something else—what had happened with Felicia Ruez? Cassidy hadn't seen her once today, and due to her flashy clothes of late, Felicia was hard to miss. But it hit Cassidy as she slid into a seat. Felicia had probably been suspended—maybe even expelled—due to what she'd posted on MyPlace. Duh.

• • ● • •

Emma confirmed it Wednesday. "This is not just idle gossip either," Emma told the DG. "It's a fact that she's been expelled. I still can't believe Felicia would do something so stupid."

Cassidy felt no satisfaction over being right about Felicia, or even for sparing the DG from being connected to her. Mostly Cassidy just felt sorry for Felicia . . . and saddened. She decided to put Felicia on her prayer list. And to add Amanda as well.

• • ● • •

The next couple days passed with no new developments. Despite an initial planning meeting for the upcoming dance, Bryn had not spoken to Amanda yet. Meanwhile, as far as Cassidy could see, Felicia had not returned to school. And no girls in the DG had made any progress in securing a date.

Knowing that midterms were around the corner and wanting to focus on academics, Cassidy put thoughts of Lane and going to the Christmas ball on the back burner. Sometimes she even toyed with the idea of dropping out of the DG altogether. As much as she liked her friends, she had a bad feeling about the direction they seemed to be taking. If Amanda—and later Amanda's friends—were going to join, things would change. Sure, Bryn and Devon and even Emma and Abby could pretend they wouldn't, but it would happen.

"I need you all to come to today's planning meeting," Bryn announced at lunch on Friday.

"I have basketball practice," Abby informed her.

"Too bad." Bryn shook her head. "It's your idea that I'm bringing up for discussion today. I hoped you'd join us."

"What idea?" Abby asked with interest.

"The fund-raiser," Bryn told her. "With some very special prizes."

"Oh?" Abby looked interested.

"I was going to ask you to chair the fund-raiser committee, Abby." Bryn sighed. "That would've looked good on college apps too."

Abby frowned. "How can I do that and basketball too?"

Bryn's brows arched. "Only you know the answer to that one, Abs." She turned to the others. "Can I count on you guys to come? This year's Christmas ball is going to be a lot more than just a dance. It's going to help local children in need to have the best Christmas ever."

"It sounds great, but how's that possible?" Cassidy asked eagerly.

"You'll have to come to the meeting to find out."

"I plan to come," Cassidy assured her. "Even more so now that I know we're not just planning a dance. I like the sound of this, Bryn."

Bryn winked at her. "You might be pleased to know that Lane will be there too. He's on the committee."

Cassidy felt her cheeks grow warm. "I was coming anyway," she said a bit testily.

Bryn pointed at Devon now. "I should warn you that Jason insisted on being on the committee too."

"Jason?" Devon scowled as she stabbed the straw into her soda cup. "Thanks for warning me. Maybe I'll take a pass on this."

"We're breaking into two committees. One to specifically plan for the dance, and the other to organize the fund-raiser," Bryn informed her. "Jason has already opted to be on the fund-raiser committee."

"Oh, right, so that means I'm stuck on the other committee?" Devon picked up her fork. "It figures that Jason gets his way. He's used to that, isn't he?"

"He is our student council president," Bryn reminded her. "And the Christmas ball is a student council event. Seems like he should be on whichever committee he chooses. But if you really want, you can be on his committee too."

"Now that would be just delightful." Devon rolled her eyes.

"Look, Devon, if it makes you feel any better, Jason seems to have changed. He doesn't seem as much like a monster as I thought. Even Amanda has quit hating him."

Devon glared at her. "I guess it's all just a matter of perspective."

"So, I should take that as a no? You will not be at the meeting?" Bryn asked her.

"I haven't made up my mind yet," Devon snapped.

"Well, at least Amanda has promised that her friends are going to help." Bryn pointed at Cassidy and Emma. "If you two are coming, that should help." She shook a finger at Abby. "Too bad you'll miss out on all the fun, Abs. Especially since it really was partly your idea."

Abby took a big bite of her burger, looking troubled. Suddenly Cassidy felt sorry for her. It wasn't fair that Abby was getting left out. "I know," she said to Abby. "How about if we figure a way for you to be involved? Maybe I could sort of represent you when you can't be at a meeting. Afterward I could send you notes and stuff and—"

"Thanks, but no thanks, Cass." Abby set down her burger and looked at them. "I already made my choice. I have to stick with it." She sighed. "At least that's what my dad says."

"But it's *your* life," Cassidy pointed out. "What if you decided it was better for you to help with the fund-raiser than to play basketball? What would be the harm in that?"

"Yeah," Devon chimed in. "What if you were playing basketball and you got hurt—like you broke a leg or something? Then you'd be out of sports for a while—all because you refused to quit a sport you didn't really want to do in the first place."

Abby made a crooked frown. "Yeah, like that's going to happen."

"You never know," Bryn said. "Think about it, Abs. Basketball isn't even your best sport. If you get scholarship money for any of your sports, you know it's going to be soccer. Why not just ditch basketball? Give yourself a break."

"But I need to stay in shape."

"So work out," Devon told her. "Take a fitness class like I'm doing."

"Or go to dance class with me," Bryn told her. "At least that's fun."

Abby looked torn. "I wish I could."

"Then just do it," Emma urged her. "Like Cass said, it's your life."

"But my dad loves coming to the games . . . when he can."

"He can still *go* to the games," Bryn told her. "It's just that you won't be playing."

Abby gave them a half smile.

"Come on, Abby," Cassidy urged. "If it was your idea to do this fund-raiser for kids, you should be involved. Think about it, what's more important—or valuable—playing a sport you're not even into or helping to raise money for needy kids to have a happier Christmas?"

"When you put it like that . . ." Abby sighed.

"It even makes me want to help out," Devon admitted. "Jason or no Jason."

"Okay!" Abby did a fist pump. "I'm in. You guys convinced me. I'm quitting basketball. Today."

They all let out some cheers and exchanged high fives. As they finished up their lunches, Cassidy had completely changed her mind again. She was into this group. The DG was a great club, and she would do all she could to keep it together and to keep it solid and good. These friendships were too valuable to cast aside.

7

Devon had been getting friendlier with Amanda and Tristin over the past week. Partly because she was grateful for their help in exposing Felicia's true colors and partly because she knew that Bryn wanted to recruit Amanda into the DG and partly because it was fun being around these pretty, popular girls—and it didn't hurt that they were a year older.

"I'm curious about something," Amanda said to Devon as they were getting dressed after their conditioning class. "You went to the homecoming dance with Jason Levine. But then you guys never went out again. Why was that?"

Devon rolled her eyes. "You mean besides the fact that Jason Levine is a low-life jerk with absolutely no respect for girls?"

"Wow." Amanda looked shocked as she pulled on a boot. "Those are pretty strong words."

"Yeah," Tristin agreed with raised brows. "What did he do anyway?"

Devon considered her answer, trying to decide how best to

play this. After all, she was aware that Jason and Amanda had been a couple for a while. She didn't want to step on Amanda's toes. "Well, that was probably an overstatement," she back-tracked. "Let's just say that Jason and I had a little disagreement that night. We decided to part ways. Mutually."

"So he's not a low-life jerk?" Tristin said with disappointment.

Devon forced a smile. "It wasn't a very fun date. Okay?"

"I have a feeling there's more to the story." Amanda laughed as she pulled on her jacket, then went over to the mirror to touch up her makeup.

"Jason thought you were a different kind of girl, didn't he?" Tristin said quietly to Devon. "He pushed you, didn't he?"

Devon made a half smile, then shrugged.

"You don't have to say it," Tristin whispered. "I knew it. Jason thought you were a Felicia type of girl, didn't he?"

Devon wasn't sure which part of this was more offensive. But she was offended. Even so, she tried to act nonchalant. "I'm not sure what he thought," she said evenly, "but we mutually decided to part ways."

"You still think he's a low-life jerk?"

"Oh, I don't know. I don't really give him much thought." Now Devon made a more genuine smile. "I think of it as just one of the many life lessons I've been learning this year." That was something that Grandma Betty—Emma's grandmother—had said to Devon recently. Something that Devon felt was true.

"That's cool." Tristin tipped her head toward where Amanda was still primping in front of the big mirror. "Because between you and me, I think Amanda is thinking about getting back together with Jason. She hasn't said as much, but I can kinda tell. And if that happens, it might not be cool if you go around calling him names."

Devon nodded gratefully. "Oh yeah. That's a good point. I really didn't mean it to sound like that. In fact, I actually agreed to be on the same committee as him for the Christmas ball." She zipped her jeans. "I'm ready to let bygones be bygones."

Tristin smiled as she fastened her belt. "I only told you that because I like you, Devon."

As she left the locker room, Devon felt a huge wave of relief. For some reason it felt important that both of these girls continued liking her, and she realized she'd almost blown it by dissing on Jason like that. She'd have to watch her step. Especially if these girls got into the DG like Bryn was recommending. But so far, no one had extended an invitation. Mostly the girls just argued about it. And, to be fair, Devon had some questions herself. Like why would Amanda, who'd had boyfriends before, need to be part of something like the DG? Bryn's argument was that Amanda was temporarily between boyfriends and that her girlfriends, Tristin and Sienna, had no boyfriends as well as no dates lined up for the Christmas ball. "They need us," Bryn had told them at the end of lunch today.

Despite the fact she'd be forced into close contact with Jason the Jerk, Devon was glad to be part of the Christmas ball committee. Still she felt apprehensive as she walked into the meeting room after school on Friday. To her relief, Jason wasn't even there. "Bryn said he's at basketball practice," Emma whispered to Devon as she took a chair next to her. "Apparently it's their first game next week and the coach laid down the law."

"Good." Devon let out a relieved sigh as Bryn began calling the meeting to order and announcing that Amanda, who was seated beside her, was going to be the co-chair for the dance.

"Thank you all for coming," Bryn said with a beaming smile. "This is going to be the best Christmas ball ever, and I'm about to tell you why." She pointed to the door that was still open. "First I want someone to close that door, and I am swearing everyone in this room to secrecy."

Naturally this got their attention, and soon Bryn was describing her plans for a very different sort of event. "As some of you may know, interest in the Christmas ball has been in a steady decline these past few years. I have several theories for why this might be—including some reluctant guys when it comes to dating in general. I think we've come up with a plan to change all that." Now she paused to introduce Abby to the group. "I have to give Abby some credit for helping me with this new idea. And I've asked her to chair the second committee."

"Second committee?" Amanda asked.

"Yes. Let me explain. The Christmas ball is going to be more than just a dance. For starters, it's going to be free."

"How can it be free?" Amanda demanded.

"Because we're going to solicit financial support from local businesses—"

"Why should local businesses donate funds for a dance?" Amanda asked.

Bryn gave her a patient smile. "If you'll just let us explain, I think you'll see how it will work." She pointed at Abby. "Why don't you tell them your idea?"

Abby stood and faced the group. "A lot of children in our city are severely impoverished. Their Christmases are usually just as bleak as the rest of their lives. Many of them go to bed hungry at night. Many don't have proper winter clothes, and most of them don't expect to get anything from Santa."

"That's really sad," Amanda admitted, "but what does it have to do with the dance?"

"Remember how I mentioned we're getting local businesses to donate funds for the dance?" Bryn asked her. "The reason they will be willing to do that is because of the number of impoverished children and families we will be reaching out to. Instead of having students buy tickets to go to the Christmas ball, they will have to earn their way by helping an impoverished child and their family during December."

"That's a sweet idea," Amanda said, "but if the guys are already not interested in going to the Christmas ball and now they have to earn their way by helping someone else—as lovely as that all sounds—why would they?"

"Because we are going to offer a big incentive," Bryn said with a twinkle in her eye. "The way that couples get into the dance is by bringing a sleigh."

"A sleigh?" Amanda frowned.

"Actually it will be a cardboard box that's decorated like a sleigh. It will be filled with whatever the couples have managed to gather to give to this child and the family for Christmas. All the sleighs will be displayed around the perimeters of the dance floor and they'll be voted on. The winners will get a fabulous prize."

"Interesting," Amanda said. "What kind of prize?"

"Well, this is the top secret part," Bryn said. "There's a chance that some very valuable tickets could be involved. It's not for certain yet, but we hope to get two tickets to the Rose Bowl and—"

Several whoops from the few guys in the room interrupted her.

"See, already we have interest," Bryn pointed out. "And those tickets will be for the guys. For the girls we hope to get something equally fun. Maybe the red carpet at the Oscars."

Now some of the girls got excited.

"Where exactly are these tickets coming from?" Amanda asked.

"We have some resources in mind." Bryn winked at Abby. "Some folks in this town with very deep pockets, if you know what I mean."

"The reason this is such a great plan," Abby said eagerly, "is that it becomes a lot more than just another dance. It's a way to help others. What better time to reach out to the less fortunate in our community than at Christmastime."

"How do we know where these so-called less-fortunates can be found?" Amanda questioned.

"We've already started to contact some outreach groups. So far they all seem eager to work with us. They have plenty of names to share," Bryn told everyone.

"I suppose it could work," Amanda conceded. "But it seems complicated to me."

"Not after you think about it for a while," Bryn told her. "There's another element we thought would be fun to add to the whole thing. We want to make it a double date night for everyone. Two couples coming together."

"We decided that the two couples will work together on one sleigh," Abby explained. "That will make the sleighs even better and take some of the pressure off."

"Since the whole event is kind of dual purposed, it makes sense to have it be a double date as well." Bryn beamed at the group. "So what do you all think? Does it sound like a fun plan?"

A few more questions were asked and answered, and enthusiasm was steadily growing. Soon it seemed that everyone was on board, and before long, they were all talking at once.

"Okay, everyone!" Bryn clapped her hands to get their attention. "We need to make two committees. One committee will be responsible for the dance in general, and I nominate Amanda Norton to head that one." She did a quick yea and nay vote and Amanda easily won. "The second committee we've decided to call Project Santa Sleigh, and I want to nominate Abby to head that one." Again she had them vote and Abby won.

"I'm not trying to turn this into a competition," Bryn told them. "But it will be interesting to see which committee puts forth the best effort. Will the Christmas ball be remembered as a fabulously fun social event, or will it be remembered as a fantastic philanthropic event that made children smile? Or better yet, will it be both? It will take everyone pitching in to make it happen."

She sent the two committee heads to separate corners of the room and challenged everyone in the room to make a decision. "Both committees are equally important," she called out as people began moving about, deciding which committee to join. "We can't do one thing without the other."

Although Devon had originally planned to be on Abby's committee, she was having a sudden change of heart. She really, really wanted to be on Amanda's committee and to work on things pertaining directly to the dance. She'd never helped with that sort of thing before—choosing a swanky location and glitzy decorations and helping to make all sorts of glamorous decisions—it sounded fun. Besides, she realized as she looked across the room, Abby already had a lot more people than Amanda. It seemed only fair.

"I'm on your team," Devon announced as she joined Amanda, Tristin, and Sienna.

"You picked the right one," Amanda told her.

Finally, after everyone had made their decisions, Bryn announced that she would continue to head up both committees. "So if anyone has any questions or suggestions or even a complaint—anything that needs special attention—feel free to come to me."

The room had gotten fairly noisy now and Amanda was having to raise her voice just to be heard. "I have an idea," she said suddenly. "How about if we move this meeting to my house? And we'll order pizza."

Naturally, everyone was on board. Devon felt even more special when Amanda offered her a ride. "Hurry," she told Devon as they headed down the hall. "I want to get home before anyone else. Just to make sure everything's in order." She laughed. "Wouldn't want to find a pair of my dad's dirty boxer shorts on the kitchen floor."

Devon laughed. Was she serious? As they were getting into Amanda's car—a sporty little blue Toyota—Devon asked about Amanda's other friends. "Don't they need a ride too?"

"They have their own cars," Amanda explained as she slipped in the key.

"Oh . . . right." Sometimes Devon forgot that most of the students at Northwood came from fairly well-off homes. Obviously Amanda and her friends did too. This became even more obvious when Amanda turned into a gated community where Devon knew some of the homes were in the million-dollar range.

"You haven't been to my house before, have you?" Amanda asked as she pulled into a circular driveway in front of a light-colored brick house.

"I don't think so." The truth was, Devon had never been here before. But she was trying to appear laid-back and unimpressed.

"Well, here we are. My parents will still be at work for a couple hours." Amanda led the way through a large covered area that reminded Devon of a hotel entrance.

"Your house is really pretty," Devon said as they went into a large foyer with stone floors and a sweeping staircase that looked like something out of a movie set.

"Home sweet home." Amanda looked around the large, immaculate room and smiled. "And no boxer shorts."

Devon laughed. "Yeah, I'll bet that happens all the time."

"If that ever happened, my mom would send the housekeeper packing." Amanda pulled out her phone and threw her bag onto a chair. "Time to order pizza."

While Amanda placed an order, Devon stared freely at the beautiful home. Everything looked expensive and carefully chosen, and it all looked like it had been taken right out of the pages of a glossy interior design magazine. Before seeing this place, Devon had thought that Bryn's house was pretty cool, but compared to this, Bryn's house was rather ordinary. Of course, Devon's house—make that her mom's house—would look like a shack next to this one. But Devon had quit thinking of her mom's house as home. Thanks to Grandma Betty, those days were behind her. Not that Grandma Betty's house was anything like this—although it was nothing to be ashamed of. Thankfully, someone like Amanda would never have to know where Devon used to live.

"There, that's settled." Amanda dropped her phone on her bag. "Want a soda or something?"

"Sure." Devon nodded, following Amanda into the kitchen. It was enormous. Probably almost as big as Devon's mom's entire house. Not that Devon wanted to think about that. "This is pretty," Devon said as she ran a hand over the sleek, cool granite countertop.

"My mom designed it," Amanda said nonchalantly as she pulled open a drawer that was really a fridge, pointing to the drinks inside. "She's got a design firm downtown. Norton's Interiors. Maybe you heard of it."

"Yeah. Maybe." Devon reached for a Coke.

"So here's what I'm thinking for the dance," Amanda said quickly. "I want it to be elegant. Formal. I'm thinking red and white."

"Red and white?" Devon was confused.

"All the girls' gowns must be red or white."

Devon considered her auburn hair and pale skin. "I don't look good in red or white."

Amanda studied her briefly. "No, you probably wouldn't. How about this? Red, white, and green."

"Green?" Devon nodded. "That works."

"Okay. Red, white, and green. Although I want it to be elegant and formal, we should keep it simple so there's not too much work. Of course, we need a photo booth." Amanda started shooting out ideas, as if she'd given this plenty of thought.

"So, you got all that?" Amanda asked as the doorbell rang.

"I guess so." Devon grinned. "Anyway, I know you do."

"Because I want you to back me," she said as she went to get the door. "You can pretend like some of the ideas are your own too. This will keep things much simpler"—she gave Devon a sly grin—"than if we let the others try to take over. You know?"

"Absolutely."

Before long their committee was settled in the family room, munching on pizza, and Amanda, with Devon's help, was tossing out ideas. Whenever others—like Tristin or Sienna—questioned anything or tried to go another direction, Devon spoke out in support of Amanda. Did she feel a bit like a puppet? Sure. But maybe it was worth it. Who better to pull her strings than someone with the kind of influence Amanda Norton had?

Emma loved the direction that the Christmas ball was going, and she was happy to help on the Project Santa Sleigh committee. But as Cassidy drove her home afterward, she felt uneasy.

"You're awfully quiet," Cassidy said as she pulled up to Emma's house. "Something wrong?"

"Sort of," Emma confessed.

"Did I say something to offend you?" Cassidy asked.

"Not this time." Emma made a stiff smile.

"Well, that's a relief." She turned to peer curiously at Emma. "What's wrong?"

"I keep thinking about Felicia," Emma admitted.

"Oh?" Cassidy frowned. "I feel bad for her too. I even put her on my prayer list. I've been asking God to turn her life around."

"What if her life doesn't need to be turned around?" Emma challenged her. "What if Felicia's the victim here?"

"Huh?"

"I studied those MyPlace photos, supposedly of Felicia—

before they were removed, that is. Something about them just seemed fake to me."

"How so?"

"They were just so cheesy looking, Cass. And the words—it was like someone was trying to set up something that looked really disgusting without crossing over a line, you know?"

"What kind of line?"

"Like a legal line. Like in case they got caught. It couldn't be called pornography. Just really bad taste."

"I don't get it. Why would someone do that?"

"I have no idea, but I want to find out if it's true."

"How is that possible?"

"I'm going to visit Felicia."

"Seriously?"

"Uh-huh. I've tried to text her and call her, but I think her phone's disconnected."

"Do you even know where she lives?"

"I know where she used to live. We used to be in Girl Scouts together. Sometimes Mom and I gave her a ride."

"Oh . . ." Cassidy looked concerned. "Are you sure you want to get involved in something like—"

"My mind is made up—I'm going." Emma looked longingly at Cassidy. "It's just that, well, I don't want to go alone."

Cassidy looked uneasy. "You want me to go with you?"

Emma nodded eagerly. "Will you?"

"Do you really believe that—that someone set Felicia up like that? That she's not the one who did it to herself?"

"I know I could be wrong," Emma confessed, "but I'd rather go talk to her and be wrong than to ignore this hunch and be right."

"Yeah . . . I can understand that."

"So will you go with me to see her?"

"When?"

"How about tomorrow morning? Not too early. Ten-ish?"

Cassidy pressed her lips together and Emma could tell she was torn. "Okay," she said finally. "I'll go too."

"Thank you!" Emma exclaimed gratefully. "I just have to get to the bottom of this. One way or another I want to know the truth, Cass."

"I know you do." Cassidy sighed. "I guess I do too now."

• • ● ● • •

By 10:00 the next morning, Emma was having second thoughts. Maybe this was crazy. Really, was she going to just go up and knock on Felicia's door? And then what? What would she say? What would she do? What if Felicia didn't want to talk? Or what if Felicia admitted she really had been the one behind all of it? Well, at least that would be the end of it, and then Emma could just put it all out of her mind.

"Ready to do this?" Cassidy asked as Emma got into her car.

"As ready as I'll ever be."

"Do you know what you're going to say?"

"Kind of."

"Well, I've been praying about this," Cassidy said as she drove. "Asking God to help us."

"Thanks."

Before long they were parked in front of Felicia's house. It was similar to Emma's house, except that it was in better condition. Like someone there cared. "I looked up their address online last night," Emma told Cassidy. "I'm pretty sure the Ruez family still lives here." She took in a deep breath. "Let's do this."

A woman who looked like an older version of Felicia answered the door. She had on a dark blue jogging suit and white athletic shoes. "Hello?" She peered curiously at them. "Are you selling something?"

"We came to see Felicia," Emma told her.

The woman narrowed her dark eyes. "What for?"

"We're worried about her," Emma said.

"Why?" the woman demanded.

"We're from Northwood," Cassidy said quickly. "We want to make sure she's doing okay."

The woman's features softened slightly. "Felicia is *not* okay."

"Can we talk to her?" Emma asked.

"Who is it, Mom?" a voice called from behind the door.

"Friends. I think." The woman scowled. "From your school."

The door swung open wide, and Felicia appeared with a dark look and her hands planted on her hips like she was ready for a fight. "Oh? Emma? And Cassidy?" She looked confused. "What are you doing here?"

"We want to talk with you," Emma said.

"Are these the ones who did this to you?" Felicia's mother demanded. "The girls that put that nasty—"

"No!" Cassidy exclaimed. "No way."

"Absolutely not," Emma added.

"Come on." Felicia grabbed their hands and tugged. "Come to my room to talk."

Once they were sequestered in Felicia's room, Emma jumped in. "I want to know the truth," she said. "Did you really put that stuff on MyPlace? Or did someone else do it to hurt you?"

"Of course someone else posted it!" Felicia said quickly. "But besides my family, no one believes me."

"You had nothing to do with it?" Cassidy asked.

"*Nothing.*" Felicia firmly shook her head. "Those pictures weren't even of me. Not the bodies anyway. Someone pasted my head onto someone else's creepy photos."

"That's what I thought too," Emma declared. "It looked totally fake to me."

"It was *all* fake. Everything they wrote too. I never said any of that stuff."

"Do you know who did it?" Cassidy asked.

Felicia slumped down into a hot-pink beanbag chair and sighed. "Not really."

"But you suspect someone?" Emma asked.

"Maybe . . ."

"We want to help you," Emma told her, "but you have to tell us everything you know."

"For starters, Felicia, can you tell us why you changed your appearance so dramatically?" Cassidy asked.

"You remember how I used to dress?" she asked them. "Well, my mom always picked out all my clothes. Sometimes I'd get teased for looking like a little girl."

"Yeah," Emma admitted. "I do remember how you mentioned that to me."

Felicia's forehead creased. "So I wanted a makeover." She looked down at her lap. "I just wanted to be more like you guys."

"*What?*" Emma was shocked. "You think we dress like . . . well, like you were doing?"

"I don't know about that, but I knew you guys figured out how to get boys to pay attention to you. You were the first ones to get dates to the homecoming dance and then to the masquerade ball. I just wanted to be like you. I wanted the boys to notice me too." She pointed at Emma. "I was so impressed by how you changed your appearance earlier in the year. Remember how I asked you about it? And we talked together . . . like we were friends. You made me think that you were going to help me too." She made a sad little sigh. "But then you didn't."

Emma bit into her lip. That was all true. Emma had acted like she wanted to help Felicia, and then she'd let her down. Big-time. "So that's why you started to dress like that?" Emma asked meekly.

"I just wanted to look pretty."

"But your clothes . . . they were so . . . well, I'm sorry to say this," Cassidy made a grimace, "but they were kinda, well, skimpy."

Felicia frowned. "Yeah, I guess so. It didn't seem like it at the time. Not to me anyway. Oh, my parents wouldn't have approved. But they'd like to keep me dressed like I'm still seven. So I had to sneak my new wardrobe to school and get dressed in the bathroom."

"You changed your clothes at school?" Emma tried to imagine Felicia dressing in the dimly lit bathroom where the mirror above the sinks only reflected from the shoulders up. Even less if you were short like Felicia. No wonder she looked so strange.

"But where did you get those clothes?" Cassidy asked.

"I studied what girls were wearing in magazines and on fashion websites. Then I bought some things online and at a thrift shop. I thought I was doing it right." Felicia pointed at Cassidy. "You changed your looks too. Remember? I just wanted to step up my game. You know?"

"I get that now," Emma told her. "That explains a lot. But we're not here to talk about your clothes. So you really did not put that crud on MyPlace? You had absolutely nothing to do with it, right?"

"That's right."

"But it's why you were expelled?"

Felicia shrugged. "First I got a warning about my clothes—the school day was almost over and I promised Mrs. Dorman that I'd wear acceptable clothes the next day. Then I got called back to the office in the middle of seventh period. I thought it was about my clothes again. But she showed me that MyPlace stuff." She choked back a sob. "I was so shocked and embarrassed. I couldn't believe it. Even when I told her and Mr. Worthington that I didn't do it, they didn't believe me. I'm sure it was because of the way I was dressed. Anyway, they called my parents and that was that."

"Do your parents believe you?"

"At first they didn't know what to think." Felicia was crying hard now. "We talked and talked and finally they accepted the truth. My dad wanted to hire a lawyer, but it's pretty expensive. Besides that, the MyPlace page got taken down so we don't even have any evidence."

"Who do you think did it?" Cassidy asked again. "Who put that stuff up? And why?"

"I don't know."

"Have you ever been threatened or bullied by anyone?" Emma asked.

"Sure. Who hasn't?"

"Who bullied you?" Cassidy pressed.

"Lots of girls . . . over the years. It's why my parents pulled me out of public school and put me into Northwood. To get away from some bully girls who just wouldn't stop." She made a sad laugh.

"But girls at Northwood bullied you too?"

"Sure."

"Who?"

"Want me to make a list?"

"Really?" Emma was surprised. "That many?"

Felicia frowned. "Maybe not that many." She held up a hand with three fingers. "I guess I can only count three." She told them three names—all that were surprising to Emma.

"Wait," Cassidy said suddenly. "Tristin Wilson bullied you?"

"Yeah."

"Why did she bully you?" Cassidy asked.

Felicia shrugged. "Who knows why? Because she's mean?"

Emma looked at Cassidy. "Why this sudden interest in Tristin anyway?"

"Don't you remember when Devon showed us the MyPlace page? Hadn't she gotten it from Tristin?"

"You honestly think Tristin put it on MyPlace?" Emma couldn't imagine that someone like Tristin would do something that low.

"It's interesting that she's the one who showed it to Devon." Cassidy turned back to Felicia. "Why do you think Tristin was picking on you?"

"I don't know . . . I guess because I'm Hispanic."

"Really?"

"That's usually part of it . . . at least that's how it feels."

"Or it could be because you're really pretty," Emma told her. "Girls might be jealous."

Felicia brightened. "You think so?"

Emma laughed. "Yeah. Everyone knows that. You're gorgeous, Felicia. That would definitely make some girls jealous. Mean girls, anyway."

"Jealous enough to make that MyPlace page?" Cassidy asked.

"Maybe." Emma was trying to wrap her head around all of this.

"Thank you guys for coming to see me," Felicia said quietly. "I know it probably won't do much good as far as Northwood goes, but it makes me feel better."

"Do you think your dad will get a lawyer?" Cassidy asked. "Because I'll bet there are some lawyers who would take this on for free. Just because it's a good case about bullying."

"I hope Dad can just forget about it. That's what I want to do."

"So you don't want to go back to Northwood?"

"Not after that." Felicia sadly shook her head. "Too humiliating."

"But you shouldn't be embarrassed," Emma told her. "Whoever did this is the one who should be humiliated. Publicly."

"Maybe we can find out who did it," Cassidy said eagerly. "I'd sure like to know."

"Me too," Emma agreed.

"Do you really think you can figure this out?" Felicia's dark eyes flickered with hope.

"I plan to do everything I can," Emma promised.

"Me too," Cassidy assured her.

"I wish we'd kept a copy of that MyPlace page," Emma said. "Then we might be able to track where it came from."

"It was only up for a few hours." Felicia sighed. "A few hours that totally ruined my life."

They talked awhile longer, but then Felicia's mom came in and announced it was time to break it up. "Felicia and I promised to have lunch with my baby sister today," she told them. "We have to get going, *mija*."

"We'll keep you posted on whatever we find out," Emma promised as she hugged Felicia good-bye on the front porch. She looked into Felicia's face. "And I just want you to know that I'm really sorry."

"You're sorry?" Felicia blinked.

Emma felt a tightness in her chest. "I'm sorry for not getting you into our . . . our club. Like I wanted to. That might've changed everything."

"Oh?" Felicia tilted her head to one side. "Were you really going to let me in?"

"I wanted you in." Emma turned to Cassidy. "Didn't I?"

Cassidy nodded with a slightly guilty expression. "Yeah . . . it's true. She did."

"In fact, I had planned to tell you that day," Emma said. "The same day that it all started to unravel for you."

Felicia made a sad little smile. "Well, it makes me feel a tiny bit better hearing that."

"I'm sorry too," Cassidy said quietly. "Truly sorry. I wish we could turn back the clock and do it all differently."

"Yeah. Me too." Felicia turned to go back into the house.

"You feel any better now?" Cassidy asked once they were in the car.

"Better . . . and worse." Emma clenched her fists. "I just wish

I knew who did that to her. I wish there was some way to pull that MyPlace page up again. But when I tried to, it was gone."

"I know. Same here. Like poof—now you see it, now you don't."

"That doesn't make sense to me," Emma declared. "People are always telling us how we need to remember that any stupid photos we post on the internet will be stuck there forever. That they can be pulled up ten years from now and keep us from getting jobs or getting into college. Not that I'd ever post something like that. But if that's true—where is the crud they created to mess up Felicia? Where did it go?"

"Good question, Em. You're right. It must still be out there somewhere. There must be a way to find it. And if we find it, there must be a way to track whoever made it," Cassidy said. "Hey, Lane is a real computer whiz. Maybe I'll ask him for help."

"Yeah, I'll bet you will." Emma poked Cassidy. "Any excuse to talk to Lane is a good excuse, right?"

"He's a very techie guy, Emma. Why shouldn't I ask him for help? Do you know someone more techie than Lane?"

"Actually, now that you mention it, Isaac is more techie than me. Maybe I'll ask him."

Cassidy giggled. "Look at us. It's like we're trying to make lemonade from lemons."

"Whatever, but I'm not giving up on this," Emma declared. "And I can't help but feel guilty, Cass. If we hadn't been so judgmental about Felicia, we could've invited her into the DG long ago—back when we started it. We would've given her a classy makeover instead of what she tried to do. And if we'd done all that, Felicia might not be in this mess right now. Or at least it might not have gotten this bad."

Emma knew that taking Felicia into the DG wasn't necessarily the magic answer to this perplexing dilemma, and it was too late for that now anyway. But she did believe there was a lesson to be learned here.

Bryn didn't know what to think when Jason texted her on Saturday morning. Because he said he had some ideas for the Christmas ball, she knew the responsible thing would be to text back. Then he asked if he could just call her.

"Sorry to interrupt your morning," he said politely. "But remember the couple I told you about. The Hartfords? The ones who might be willing to donate the prizes for the dance?"

"Of course. You said they'd have access to Rose Bowl and red carpet tickets." She didn't tell him that she'd felt skeptical about this from the start.

"Well, you didn't mention them at the meeting yesterday, did you?"

"Actually I did—"

"No!" he exclaimed. "That could ruin everything. Jack Hartford explicitly told me that he didn't want their name involved and—"

"I didn't say their names," Bryn clarified, "I just mentioned

Melody Carlson

that we might have those tickets for the prize. Everyone got really excited too."

"Oh . . . well, that's okay."

"Are the Hartfords really going to donate them?" Bryn knew who the Hartfords were by name only. They owned a successful software corporation and were reputed to be the richest couple in the state.

"That's why I'm calling. Jack and Beth have invited us to their house for lunch. They want to talk to us about this whole thing in person."

Bryn was so excited she was dancing around her bedroom. Even so she kept her voice calm. "We're invited to their home? For lunch?"

"Yeah, that's what I said. I'm so glad you didn't drop their name yesterday. That would've ruined this. Can you come?"

"Uh, sure, I think so. What time?"

"Beth said around 1:00."

"Oh . . . okay. That works." Bryn suppressed a giggle. Like she wouldn't have cleared her "busy schedule" completely for a chance to have lunch at the Hartfords' home.

"How about if I pick you up?"

She considered this.

"Or if you want to meet me there, I can give you directions. It's a little out of town, kinda in the country. When you get there you'll have to wait at the gates and call for security and—"

"That's okay," she said quickly. "I'll just ride with you."

"I'll pick you up about 12:45 then."

She wanted to ask what she should wear, but that just sounded so lame and juvenile. After all, Bryn considered herself something of a fashion expert. She ought to be able to figure this one out for herself. Instead, she politely thanked him and hung up. She had exactly two hours to do her hair and makeup and pick out the perfect outfit.

"What are you getting all dolled up for?" Bryn's mom asked as Bryn walked through the kitchen wearing hot rollers and a facial mask.

"You'll never believe it," Bryn told her as she got a glass of water.

"Try me."

So Bryn explained about the charity event and how the Hartfords might contribute the prizes. "For some reason they want us to come to their home today. I guess they want to hear more about this project."

"That's just wonderful, Bryn." Mom smiled. "I'm so impressed."

"I wanted to look really good." Bryn frowned down at her pajama pants and T-shirt. "But I'm having a hard time deciding what to wear. I definitely don't think jeans are appropriate— although their house is in the country."

Mom got a thoughtful look. "Something classic would probably be a safe choice." She glanced out the window. "It's getting cold out there. Maybe it calls for some cashmere? Perhaps a scarf?"

Bryn beamed at her. "Yeah, I was thinking along those same lines. Maybe my new Lucky boots and a matching belt. Kind of country cool."

Mom laughed. "You better tell me about everything when you get home. I'd suggest you take photos of their home, but I'm afraid that'd be rude. Just take mental notes."

"I'd love to take photos, but you're right. I won't even ask. Bad manners."

"Good girl."

"Where's Dad?"

"He has a meeting in town." Mom patted Bryn on the back. "I'm sure he'll be very impressed to hear who you've been lunching with."

Bryn remembered what Jason had said. "Don't tell anyone about this, okay? For some reason the Hartfords seem like they want to keep their donations under wraps. I'm so glad I didn't mention their names yesterday. Although I did tell Abby. I better call her and make sure she hasn't blabbed about it to anyone."

"I wouldn't be concerned." Mom filled her coffee cup. "Abby's never been much of a blabbermouth."

"Even so." Bryn hurried to her room for her phone and quickly called Abby, explaining what was happening today and the need to keep it secret.

"Don't worry," Abby told her. "The only person I told was my dad. And it was only to get him off my case for quitting basketball."

"He's pretty mad about that?"

"Oh yeah."

"Sorry, Abs. I'm sure he'll get over it."

"Maybe by the time I head off for college."

"Isn't he impressed with the charity event that you're helping with? You're the chairman of the committee, Abs. That should wow him."

"You'd think. He was good with that, but he thought I should be able to do both. I mean, I should do it all, right? He lectured me about all the committees and sports and jobs he'd juggled while going to high school. And how he had to walk ten miles in blizzards . . . and weave his own clothes . . . and hunt his own food. Back in the Dark Ages."

Bryn laughed.

"So you're going to the Hartfords' house?" Abby asked with a tinge of longing in her voice.

"Yeah." Bryn suddenly felt guilty. Should she invite Abby? "I was pretty surprised by it myself, but Jason sounds all laid-back and—"

"Jason is going too?" Abby sounded shocked.

"Yeah. The Hartfords are friends with his family. Jason is our connection to them."

"Oh . . . I wonder why they want it kept hush-hush," Abby mused.

"Probably just a rich-person thing." Bryn started wiping off her facial mask with tissues. "They might not want everyone hitting them up for fund-raisers. From what Jason said, it sounds like they've been supportive of Northwood. Their kids went there about ten years ago."

"Well, I'll be curious to hear what they're like. Call me when you get back, okay?"

"Absolutely." Bryn dropped a gooey tissue in the wastebasket. "Sorry I couldn't invite you to come too, Abs, but you understand . . ."

"Sure."

Bryn continued doing her hair and makeup and carefully dressed, checking her image over and over to be sure everything was perfect. She'd never had lunch with mega-millionaires before. For all she knew they might be billionaires.

"You look very nice," Mom said as Bryn came out to show her the outfit she'd decided on. "That blue sweater brings out your eyes, and the scarf looped like that is quite stylish."

"What about the skinny khakis tucked into the boots?" Bryn asked. "Too equestrian?"

"Perfect. You look like a stylish girl off to the country for a nice lunch." Mom grabbed her iPhone. "Let me get a pic of you to show Dad." She'd just taken it when the doorbell rang.

"That's Jason Levine. He's going too."

"Have fun, sweetie."

Bryn grabbed her suede jacket and hurried to get the door.

"Don't you look swanky," he said with a pleased smile.

"Swanky?"

"Okay. Chic. Is that better?"

Melody Carlson

"A little." As she closed the front door, she noticed the car pulled into the driveway. A small black BMW that looked fairly new. "Is *that* yours?"

"My mom's. She insisted."

"Nice ride." Bryn kept her expression even, but she could feel herself getting swept away as she slid into the smooth leather seat. As much as she tried to pretend she was not a "material girl," these little luxuries did tend to turn her head.

"I was planning on driving my Jeep," he said as he started the engine, "but my mom noticed how dirty it was. She couldn't stand to have me park it in front of the Hartfords'." He laughed. "I reminded her that the Hartfords have horses and cows, but she still put her foot down."

"Good for her," Bryn said. "I like your mom's car." She was aware that Jason was from a fairly well-off family, but now she was wondering, just how rich were they? And to be such good friends with people like the Hartfords? Was it possible that she'd underestimated this boy? Sure, there was that mess with Devon that night. But what if Devon had been partially to blame? And, really, would that surprise her? Devon hadn't proved herself to be the most trustworthy or reliable girl, had she?

"You're being so quiet," he said as he turned onto the highway.

"Sorry . . . just thinking."

"Worrying that I might drag you off into the woods and try to have my way with you?"

She jerked her head around to stare at him.

"Sorry," he said quickly. "Just yanking your chain. I mean, after what you said about Devon and all that. I figure you still assume that I'm a—what did you call me—a *cad*?"

She smiled. "As a matter of fact . . ."

"Hopefully, you'll get to know me for yourself . . . for who I really am."

She studied him. With his chocolate-brown sweater over a pale blue oxford shirt, combined with tan cords and loafers, he not only looked casually stylish and handsome, he looked perfectly harmless too. Still, she knew that looks could be deceiving.

"So tell me about the Hartfords. How do your parents know them?"

"Didn't I tell you?"

"Not that I recall."

"Jack and my uncle Dan started the company back in the mid-nineties. My dad joined the team after college. He's a few years younger than Jack."

"Oh." So Jason's family was part of the company. That meant they probably were very wealthy. Not that it mattered. Or did it? After a nice drive down a country road, Jason turned onto a road that had tall metal gates. He punched something into the keypad and—voila—the gates swung open.

"Beth loves horses," Jason told her as he slowly drove down the gravel road. "She's got about a dozen I think. Mostly Arabians, but I heard she's getting interested in Friesians—whatever those are."

"Friesians? They just happen to be one of the most beautiful breeds. Big, shiny black draft horses. They're gorgeous."

"Sounds like you know a little about horses." He was pulling up to an enormous house. It resembled a castle in that it was made of stones, but it was long and low and more modern looking, with lots of big windows.

"Pretty house," she said as he turned off the engine.

"Pretty big," he said as they got out of the car. "It's about twelve thousand square feet."

"Wow." She took in a deep breath, steadying herself for whatever was ahead. It felt like she was about to visit royalty. Perhaps she should've practiced her curtsy.

"Welcome," called out a short redheaded woman as she opened the double doors. "Watch out for the dogs." Just then a pair of golden retrievers burst out the door, racing up to Jason and Bryn. "Stay down!" the woman yelled as she hurried over. "Down, Riley. Down, Roxie."

"Hey, Beth," Jason hugged the woman. "I want you to meet Bryn."

Beth stuck out her hand, and Bryn tried not to look disappointed as she shook it. So much for visiting royalty. This ordinary woman in her faded blue jeans, frumpy gray sweatshirt, and scuffed up boots wasn't even as fashionable as Bryn's mom . . . or even her grandmother. "I'm pleased to meet you," Bryn said with a big smile.

"Excuse my appearance," Beth said. "I was working with a new horse and sort of lost track of the time."

"A Friesian?" Bryn asked.

"Yes. How did you know?"

"Jason mentioned it. I think they're one of the most beautiful breeds."

Beth's eyebrows arched. "So you're a horsewoman?"

Bryn gave her an embarrassed smile. "I was pretty horse crazy as a girl. I took riding lessons for a few years and dreamed of having a horse, but I've never owned one."

"Then I'll have to give you a tour of the stables. That is, if you're interested."

"Absolutely." Suddenly Bryn began to see this woman in a new light.

"Jack's inside," Beth told them, "and I know he's hungry. Plus he's only got about an hour to spend with us because there's a brokers' meeting at three."

She led them into the huge and amazing house. It wasn't that it was so fancy or elaborate. The furnishings actually looked comfortable and casual, but the vaulted wood ceilings, the enormous fireplace that opened into two rooms, and all the gleaming wood floors—well, it was pretty stunning. "You have a beautiful home," Bryn told Beth as they were led to a large, sunny room with several comfortable looking chairs. A dining table was beautifully set with colorful place mats, pottery, and flowers.

"Thank you," Beth said. "I never dreamed I'd have a house this big. Thankfully, I don't have to clean it. You kids make yourselves comfy. I'll send Rita in with some drinks while I round up Jack and do a quick change out of my horse clothes."

"I love this house," Bryn whispered to Jason as they sat down in the chairs by the window.

"It's pretty cool."

"And Beth seems nice."

"Yeah, she is."

"Not at all what I expected."

"What did you—"

"Hello there," called out an athletic-looking gray-haired man. "Beth told me you kids were here. Welcome."

Jason introduced Jack to Bryn, and she gave him her brightest smile. "Thank you. Your home is beautiful. Everything about it. Feels like a lot of good energy went into it."

He grinned. "That's true. We wanted it to feel more like a home than a showplace. Had to fire several designers until we found someone who could understand that." He waved to the table as a woman came in with a couple pitchers of beverages. "Let's sit down and chat."

Before long, Beth was back. Dressed in a loose cream-colored shirt and black pants, she looked stylish and comfortable. As she sat down at the opposite end from her husband, Bryn realized that she was actually quite pretty and not so frumpy after all.

Before they ate, Jack bowed his head and asked a short blessing on the food. Bryn wasn't sure why this surprised her, but for some reason it did. Maybe it was because her family—though churchgoing—rarely prayed before a meal. But she liked it. And she liked Jack and Beth. As she and Jason presented their plan for helping local children in need, via the Christmas ball, she could see that the Hartfords were engaged and interested, and they seemed like truly good people. She could tell that they were buying wholeheartedly into this plan. By the time dessert was being served, Bryn felt completely comfortable with these people. She could even imagine living comfortably in their world.

don't see why Dad's being so stubborn," Abby said to her mom on Monday morning as she gathered her things for school. "Why can't he just let it go?"

"He just loves you, Abby. Wants the best for you."

"You mean what he thinks is best." She zipped her bag shut. "I wish he'd just let me grow up and run my own life."

"Well, eventually he'll have to, won't he?" Mom kissed Abby on the cheek. "In the meantime, try to be patient."

"What happens when my patience wears out?"

"Then you'll have to ask God for more."

Abby looked out the window to see Bryn's car. "Gotta go." She grabbed her jacket and sprinted for the door. She wanted to get out of here before Dad returned from his morning run. She continued running out to the car, hurrying to hop in.

"What's the big rush?" Bryn asked.

"Trying to escape the wrath of Dad," Abby explained as she buckled up. "We had a little blowup before he went running. I don't really want to pick it up where we left off."

"Got ya." Bryn nodded as the car pulled out. "Want me to take a special route to avoid him?"

"That's not necessary."

"You never called me back on Saturday," Bryn said as she drove. "I wanted to tell you about my visit to the Hartfords'."

"Didn't you get my text saying my parents suddenly decided we should spend the weekend at the mountain cabin?"

"Yeah. But I just wanted to talk to you." Bryn proceeded to describe in detail how fabulous the Hartford estate was. She even described the horses.

"Sounds lovely," Abby said without real interest.

"Remember, you can't tell anyone about them. Their gift must remain anonymous. It's the way they do things."

"That's nice." Abby knew her voice sounded flat, but she didn't really care.

"What's wrong, Abs?"

"Nothing." Abby folded her arms across her front, slumping into the seat with a long, loud sigh.

"Yeah, right." As Bryn stopped for a red light, she turned to peer at Abby. "Come on, something is bugging you. What's up?"

"My dad is driving me nuts. First of all, he just won't let it go that I quit basketball. In fact, I know that's why they kidnapped me to the cabin. They thought they could brainwash me up there."

"Did it work?"

"To be honest, it did give me some second thoughts."

"You really want to go back to basketball? Forget about the Christmas project?"

"Jason is managing to do both," Abby pointed out. This was a little fact that she hoped Dad never discovered. "I probably can too."

"Jason is an expert at delegating. He likes being up in front, getting others to do the hard work. That in turn leaves him more time to play ball."

"Maybe that's what I should do." But even as she said this, she knew it wouldn't work.

"But we need you to do the hard work too," Bryn argued. "You've got great organizational skills. The Santa Sleigh project is going to need them." Bryn started to explain how generous the Hartfords were planning to be. "They're giving us Rose Bowl tickets and red carpet Oscars tickets. Two of each. They also promised to help in some other ways too. Beth knows the owners of Ice Capers. She thinks we can have a skating party there for the kids, and at the end of it, we'll have a Santa show up and present them with their sleighs. Can you imagine how cool that would be—to have all the sleighs on ice?"

Abby brightened. "That would be fun for the kids."

"Beth helped us come up with some really great ideas, ways to help the kids with a lot of things. I've got a bunch of notes."

"The big challenge will be to get everyone at school on board," Abby said. "I was wondering if they'd let us have a short assembly—just to get everyone excited, you know?"

"Fantastic idea, Abby. See, this is just one more reason why you need to stick to your guns and scrap basketball and stay with our project."

"So I'm thinking . . ." Abby closed her eyes. "How about if we make a couple of cardboard-box sleighs. You know, like we talked about. We'd go all out to decorate them—maybe even use lights. Then we could have a couple of girls—ones that are pint-sized—dress up like a pair of goofy-looking elves and pull the sleighs out on the stage. And you could tell everyone about the contest and how it will benefit kids."

"Elves and sleighs—how adorable!"

"Then, of course, you could tell everyone about the dance and the double-date plan and finally—announce the prizes."

"That settles it, Abby. You don't belong on the basketball team. We need you on our team. You've got fabulous ideas and you're great at organizing. Please, promise me you won't quit us. Even if you do decide to play basketball."

"No, I'm not going to play basketball. I've made up my mind. That was Dad's dream. Not mine. It was fun in middle school, and for the first year in high school. But after that, it got too serious. I told the coach that I quit last week and I'm sticking to it." Abby grinned at Bryn. "Thanks for helping me to see I made the right decision."

• • ● • •

By noon, Abby had a couple more ideas for the assembly. "I think we should have some live music," she told Bryn as they walked into the cafeteria. "You know how Kent has his band? I asked him if he'd be interested and he was jazzed. He said they could do some fun Christmas number. Maybe alter the lyrics to match the event. Like 'The Twelve Days of Christmas.' He's going to talk to his band guys about it."

"Well, they'll have to get on it fast. I talked to Mr. Worthington and he's scheduled the assembly for Friday afternoon."

Abby pulled out her phone. "I'll let Kent know."

"Cool."

"We need to talk," Cassidy said urgently, tugging them both by the arm toward their usual table.

"Can we at least grab something to eat?" Abby asked.

Bryn held up her brown bag. "And I want a soda."

"Just be quick," Cassidy commanded.

"Don't say a word about whatever it is until we get there," Bryn told Cassidy. She and Abby hurried into the line, which fortunately was short. While Bryn headed for the soda machine and saved a place in line at the cashier, Abby grabbed a chef salad and some apple juice. She handed it to Bryn along with her money and within seconds they were back at the table.

"What's up?" Abby asked breathlessly.

"Tell them," Cassidy commanded Devon.

"I invited Amanda to join the DG," Devon said with an expression that looked partly proud and partly sheepish.

"*What?*" Bryn slammed her soda cup onto the table. "That was my job."

"Says who?"

"We voted on it," Bryn reminded her.

"We voted to let Amanda into the club," Devon argued. "Not about who could or could not ask her. Besides Amanda and I are good friends now. It was more natural for me to ask her. I was at her house and we got to talking. What's the big deal?"

Abby shrugged. "I don't think it's a big deal."

"Well, I feel kind of blindsided," Bryn said.

Devon made a genuine-looking sympathetic expression. "I'm so sorry, Bryn. I actually thought you'd be glad about this. Isn't it great? We have enough girls for the double date now. In fact, Amanda and I have decided that we'll pair off. I figured no one here would mind." She laughed. "Especially since I'm kinda the black sheep anyway."

Bryn made a half smile. "Yeah, I guess it's okay. But maybe you should've called me about it. You know?"

"Okay," Cassidy announced loudly. "Now that you've heard about that, Em and I have another interesting news flash."

"What?" Bryn asked.

"Go ahead," Cassidy urged Emma. "It's really your story."

Emma set her fork down and looked from face to face, as if her news was fairly serious. "It's about Felicia Ruez. Cass and I went to see her this weekend and it turns out that she had nothing to do with that disgusting MyPlace page."

"That's too bad," Devon said. "But what does it have to do with us?"

"A lot," Emma told her. "For starters, you shared that page with us, Devon, remember?"

"Yeah . . . ?"

"And it turns out that we're partly to blame for the skanky makeover that Felicia gave herself," Cassidy told them.

"That's just plain ridiculous," Bryn declared.

"Not really." Emma explained Felicia's flawed reasoning and how she dressed in the bathroom before school.

"Man, that is totally pathetic," Devon said.

"I feel sorry for her," Abby admitted.

"So do I," Cassidy told them. "We want to help her."

"How?" Bryn asked.

"I'm not sure," Emma said. "But we need everyone's help. Remember how Devon and Cassidy went looking for evidence that Felicia wasn't DG material? We all need to look for evidence of whoever made that bogus MyPlace page."

"The tricky part is that no one seems to have downloaded it," Cassidy explained. "Not even the school."

"Mrs. Dorman was so outraged that she called up MyPlace, and they took it down so fast that no one ever thought to download it for evidence." Emma shook her head. "I've asked Isaac to look into it, but so far he's come up with nothing."

"We want everyone to keep their ears and eyes wide open. If you hear anyone say anything about Felicia, pay attention." Cassidy looked over her shoulder as if she was concerned someone was listening.

"And ask around," Emma said. "Without sounding too suspicious, try to find out if anyone possibly saved a download." She pointed to Devon. "It looks like you've got the inside track with Tristin and Amanda. Try to find out how they discovered the page. Who sent it to them? And why?"

"Okay, okay." Bryn held up her hands. "I totally understand your concern, Emma. It's really sad that this happened to Felicia. But we cannot let her little mess distract us. Don't forget we have a big project ahead—a project that's meant to benefit needy children in our town." Bryn explained the plan for the assembly, eventually passing the conversation over to Abby.

"We'll need to make a couple of really fun and flashy sleds." Abby pointed to Emma. "You're the artist of the group. Can you help to direct this?"

"Sure." Emma nodded. "Sounds like fun."

"And we need a couple of petite girls to dress up like elves." Abby pointed at Emma again. "You're an obvious choice, but I hate putting everything on you."

"I'll help you get costumes together," Bryn told Emma. "We can hit up the drama department for something fun."

"I'll help with the sleighs," Cassidy offered. "I'm not as artsy as Emma, but I know how to cut and glue stuff and follow directions."

"I could put together some fake presents for the sleighs," Abby said. "Wait—maybe it would be more effective to have the sleighs empty. The elves could be acting all sad, like the children aren't going to get any presents."

"Great idea." Bryn patted Abby on the back. "See why you're chairing that committee?"

"How about if we just have one sleigh for the assembly?" Emma suggested. "A really nice one. That might make it seem more dramatic—a big fancy sleigh with nothing in it."

They all agreed. Then, continuing to toss around more ideas, they also made plans for some after-school work meetings. Just as the bell rang, Bryn reminded them that the assembly was on Friday.

"This is going to be the best Christmas ball ever," she told everyone. "Go team!"

As Abby walked toward the science department, she felt glad for the decision she'd made. She would much rather be working together on something like this with her good friends than sweating on the basketball court. Even if her dad couldn't understand it right now, perhaps he would get it when he saw all the good they were going to do—all the young lives they were going to touch with their generosity. At least she hoped he would.

"Devon doesn't want a ride home?" Cassidy asked Emma as they met in the locker bay after school. "I mean, uh, to your grandmother's house."

"It's okay. Devon calls it home too," Emma clarified. "And, no, she doesn't need a ride. She's with Amanda."

"She and Amanda are getting to be pretty good friends, huh?"

"Apparently." Emma sounded slightly aggravated.

"You don't like that they're friends?" Cassidy wondered if Emma was jealous. She and Devon used to be good friends, but that seemed to have deteriorated recently.

Emma slammed her locker shut. "I'm not sure."

"You have a problem with Amanda?" Cassidy glanced around to make sure no one was listening.

"Maybe."

The truth was, Cassidy wasn't too keen on the news that Amanda Norton was a member of the DG. It had felt rather sudden and slightly underhanded. Sure, they needed an even number of members, but shouldn't they have discussed it more?

"What are you thinking in regard to Amanda?" Cassidy asked Emma after they were outside and nearly to her car.

"I'm thinking that it was Amanda and Tristin who first showed Devon that MyPlace page on Felicia. Remember?"

"Yeah."

"And Felicia said that Tristin was one of the girls who'd teased her."

"Yeah?"

"Amanda and Tristin are really good friends. At least they used to be."

"Uh-huh." Cassidy unlocked her car. This wasn't really news. "Your point is what?"

"Well, I know it's not enough evidence to convict anyone, but it seems suspicious. Just a few minutes ago when I asked Devon if she'd found out anything—because remember how we asked her to do some sleuthing with Amanda and Tristin—she got all defensive." Emma scowled as she slammed the door closed. "What's up with that?"

"What do you mean defensive? Who's she defending? Amanda? Tristin? Herself?"

"I'm not sure, but she got pretty irate. Like I had no business questioning any of them. She told me that just because Felicia claimed she hadn't put up that page didn't mean it was true."

"So she still thinks Felicia is like that?" Cassidy started her car.

"Who knows what she thinks. She's being awfully protective of her new friends, though."

Suddenly Cassidy remembered something she'd seen in the math department earlier. "Speaking of Tristin . . . have you noticed that she seems to be in hot pursuit of Marcus Zimmerman?"

"No. Why do you mention it?"

"Because I remember seeing Marcus literally tripping over himself with his eyes on Felicia."

"Huh? What do you mean?"

"I mean Felicia had caught Marcus's eye. Then today I saw Tristin blatantly flirting with the boy. Do you think there's any connection?"

Emma was pulling out her phone. "I'm texting Felicia now. Asking her about Marcus."

"What are you asking?"

"If she thinks Marcus was into her." Emma tapped away.

"It seems like a pretty wimpy theory," Cassidy admitted.

"Well, at least you're trying." Emma held up her phone to show she was done. "Unlike Devon."

"Devon is probably trying to protect her new friendship with Amanda," Cassidy said as she came to a stop sign. She turned to Emma. "To be honest, I'm surprised that Amanda was into being Devon's friend. What do you think that's about?"

Emma shrugged. "I have no idea. Hey, Felicia texted back. In all caps she said YES."

"Yes to Marcus?"

"Uh-huh. I think so." Emma was texting again. "How about if we stop by her house since we're so close anyway?"

"Okay." Cassidy turned down the next street. "That way I can hear it too."

"I'll tell her we're coming."

Before long, they were back in Felicia's bedroom and she was telling them about how she and Marcus had started a friendship about a month ago. "He was helping me with math and being really nice about it. I guess I kinda hoped it was more than just friendship. I had wanted him to ask me out." Felicia gave an embarrassed smile. "He was one of the main reasons I wanted to step up my game in the fashion arena. Although I obviously just made a mess of everything." Her smile faded.

"Remember the time Marcus fell down in Algebra II?" Cassidy said suddenly. "Everyone laughed and he made a bow?"

"Yeah." She nodded. "I do."

"Well, I saw the whole thing. Marcus had been looking at you and didn't even see the chair right in front of him," Cassidy explained. "The boy seemed somewhat smitten."

Felicia giggled then grew serious. "Not that it does me any good now. I went back to public school today. I hate it."

"I'm curious," Emma said. "On what grounds did you get expelled from Northwood?"

"Because of MyPlace," Felicia said with a "duh" expression. "Remember?"

"I know. But what do they have as evidence?"

Felicia frowned. "Good question."

"It doesn't seem fair that they can keep you out of school without a shred of evidence—especially considering it's something you didn't even do," Emma declared.

"Yeah," Cassidy agreed. "What happened to innocent until proven guilty? How can they prove you guilty of anything—well, besides bad taste in clothes—without any evidence?"

"I wish you guys were my lawyers," Felicia said wistfully.

"Maybe we'll do that," Cassidy told her.

"Huh?" Emma looked curiously at Cassidy.

"What if we tried to present her case to Mr. Worthington and Mrs. Dorman?"

"What would we say?" Emma asked.

"We'd have to prepare some kind of statement. It would be nice if we had some kind of evidence." Cassidy held a finger in the air. "So back to Tristin. You mentioned her as one of the girls who has harassed—or bullied —you, right?"

Felicia nodded somberly. "Yeah. It took me by surprise too. Kinda out of nowhere. The other girls who were mean—well, they were just flat-out mean, and to be honest, it wasn't that big of a deal. They don't seem like they're very happy with themselves or life in general, you know? It was easier to forgive them. But when Tristin jumped in . . . well, that felt more personal. You know?"

Cassidy remembered the other two girls Felicia had named. Both of them were kind of outsiders and not well liked by anyone. Not that it meant they should be bullies, but Felicia—since it was her first year at Northwood—had probably seemed an easy target.

"What did Tristin do exactly?" Emma asked.

"She went onto my MyPlace page—my real one—and said some mean, trashy stuff about me."

"Really?" Cassidy asked eagerly. "Do you still have it?"

"They took that page down too," Felicia explained. "They didn't even ask me. Just took it down."

"And you never downloaded it?"

Felicia got a thoughtful look. "Actually, I think I did, but I'm not sure if I still have it. I hadn't actually given it much thought. I mean, it wasn't like she'd done anything illegal or—"

"Can you pull it up?" Cassidy asked.

Felicia already had the laptop and was punching the keys. "I'll see."

"When did Tristin do this?" Emma asked her. "Can you remember?"

"It started about a month or so ago." Felicia continued keyboarding.

"Did you know that Tristin likes Marcus?" Cassidy asked as she and Emma stood looking over Felicia's shoulder.

Felicia turned around to stare at them. "No way."

"It's true," Cassidy assured her. "I saw Tristin flirting with him today. I could tell she was pretty serious about it too. I'm guessing she's trying to warm him up to take her to the Christmas ball."

"I have Sienna in art," Emma said, "and she said that she and Tristin are making a sleigh together. So they're obviously planning to go to the dance as a double date."

"A sleigh? Double date? Huh?" Felicia was confused.

"TMI." Cassidy pointed at the laptop. "Just see if you can

find the MyPlace page, Felicia. That could be your ticket back into Northwood."

"Really?" She turned back around and continued looking. "Aha!" she cried out. "Here it is."

Emma and Cassidy leaned over to see better. "Do not delete this under any circumstances," Cassidy told her. "In fact, why don't you email it to me and Emma right now?"

Felicia's fingers flew over the keys. "There. Done." She turned looking hopefully up at them. "What next?"

"Good question." Cassidy sat down on Felicia's bed, pulling out her iPad to be sure the email had gone through.

"We need to do like you said," Emma told her. "To present Felicia's case to Worthington and Dorman."

"And we need to do it in such a way that they take us seriously," Cassidy added.

"You guys would really do that for me?" Felicia looked close to tears.

"You bet we would," Cassidy assured her as she skimmed over the MyPlace page. "These comments from Tristin are proof of bullying. If she was after Marcus and jealous of his interest in you, well, it's not looking good for that girl."

"Hey, I just remembered something Isaac told me today," Emma said suddenly. "If we found the computer that originated the MyPlace page, we might find evidence."

"If we could figure out what Tristin used . . ." Cassidy was thinking out loud. "Whether it was an iPhone or iPad or laptop or whatever . . . and if we could get our hands on it . . . we might be able to prove she did it."

"Do you really think you can?" Felicia asked eagerly. "If it's possible, can you please do it soon? The sooner I get back to school, the better it will be for my grades and my classes."

"We'll do our best," Emma promised as they told Felicia good-bye.

"And we'll be in touch," Cassidy told her.

"Interesting development," Emma said as they got back into Cassidy's car.

"Yeah. I think we've found our culprit."

"The question is, can we get the evidence to take her down?"

"I've never liked Tristin that much," Cassidy admitted, "but I never would've guessed she'd do something so despicable. Did you read the nasty, mean stuff Tristin wrote on Felicia's page?"

"And all over a boy? What's next? Murder?"

Cassidy shuddered. "Creepy."

"I hope we didn't get Felicia's hopes up too much. It seems like a somewhat daunting challenge, now that I think about it. Seriously, Cass, how are we going to pry an iPhone or iPad or laptop out of Tristin's grubby little hands?"

"Maybe Devon can help," Cassidy suggested. "If we could get the whole DG on this, we might actually have—"

"The *whole* DG?" Emma let out a groan. "Amanda too?"

"I guess this won't be easy."

"Time to change the subject," Emma said as Cassidy pulled up to her house. "We need to figure out when we can get together to work on our sleigh. I want it to look really, really great. Not just for the assembly but for the contest too. I'd start working on it today if I had the right kind of box."

"What kind of box do we need?" Cassidy asked.

Emma held her hands far apart. "A great big one."

"Hey, my dad got a new printer delivered to our house over the weekend. It came in a really big box. If it's still in the garage, I'll scavenge it if you want."

"Great. Can you bring it over here?"

"Sure. But I have homework so I can't help with it much."

"That's okay. For starters I'll just try to shape it into something. Maybe give it a first coat of paint. Then I'll sketch out some design options and get your input. By then maybe you'll be ready to help."

"Cool."

"Does this mean we're partnering up for the double date for the Christmas ball?" Emma asked hopefully.

"I'd like that," Cassidy admitted. "I was going to ask you, but it's not like either of us have dates yet."

"We will," Emma said with confidence.

Cassidy laughed. "We've come a long way since the beginning of school."

"With a long way still to go."

Cassidy promised to return shortly with the box. As she continued on home, she realized that because she and Emma had partnered up, Bryn and Abby would be forced to do the same. Not that they should mind. After all, they'd been best friends for ages. Just the same, she would be sure to send them a text with this news.

Cassidy was relieved to be doing this with Emma. Abby would've been her second choice, and that probably would've gone okay. She wasn't too sure if she and Bryn would've gotten along that well though. Bryn could be pretty bossy at times. Cassidy's biggest fear had been getting stuck with Devon. Although she'd been trying to be a better friend to Devon lately, the idea of being partnered with her on a project like this—and for a double date—well, that had been a little scary.

Devon was truly grateful for the way that Grandma Betty had invited her into her home. Devon had been trying her best to comply with Grandma Betty's rules and to be helpful and sociable and responsible. But sometimes she felt a bit over-whelmed by the old woman's expectations. To always get home in time—not only to eat dinner but to help prepare it—and to obey an early curfew as well as to keep up with the assigned chores that Grandma Betty kept posted on the fridge . . . It sometimes felt a little like boot camp. But Devon told herself it was worth it. Plus she believed that Grandma Betty really cared about her. It felt like she had Devon's best interests at heart. That was worth a lot.

Besides, Devon reminded herself as she peeled carrots, it was better than living in a small, run-down house where slimy Rodney could show up whenever he pleased and stay as long as he liked. Out of curiosity, Devon had ridden her bike past her old house on Sunday and there, sure enough, was that big, ugly red truck parked in the driveway like he owned the place.

Well, fine—he could have it if he wanted. She pretended like she didn't care . . . but it still hurt.

"I'd like to meet your new friend," Grandma Betty said as she poured chicken broth into a pot. "What's Amanda's last name?"

"Norton."

"Norton?" Grandma Betty got a thoughtful look. "Is that the same Nortons who own the dry-cleaning business?"

"No. Amanda's dad is an attorney for the city, and her mom is an interior designer." Devon could feel the pride in her voice as she shared this information. She'd never had a good friend with parents this impressive before. It felt good.

"They sound very interesting." Grandma Betty slid the chopped potatoes into the pot. "Have you met her parents yet?"

"Not yet, but I've been in their house." Devon described how beautiful the Norton home had been. She'd wanted to tell someone about this before, but none of her friends seemed interested. And she hadn't wanted to make Grandma Betty feel bad—as if Devon thought that Amanda's house was so much grander than here. Even if it was.

"Her parents must be very wealthy."

"Oh yeah. They are."

"Do you think that being wealthy is very important?"

"It beats being poor."

Grandma Betty chuckled. "Yes, I can understand that."

"I plan on being rich someday."

"If you had to choose, which would you rather be—rich or happy?"

Devon dropped the last peeled carrot in the bowl. "Well, if I was rich, I think I would be happy."

"I wonder if Amanda's parents are happy." Grandma Betty started to chop the carrots.

"Why wouldn't they be? They have everything."

"Maybe, but I've noticed something over the years. Some people—not all of course, but I've known people who have a lot of material wealth—also have a lot of stress and obligations attached to their holdings. Sometimes I've wondered, when it's all weighed out, is it worth it? Especially when they don't seem particularly happy most of the time."

Devon considered this. "Yeah, well, I'm sure that some rich people aren't happy. But I doubt they'd be any happier if they were poor."

"Good point." Grandma Betty grinned at her. "You're a smart girl, Devon. I'm sure you'll figure these things out."

• • ● • •

After dinner, Devon was surprised to hear the doorbell ring. Grandma Betty didn't usually get callers at night. Thinking it was one of Betty's friends, Devon continued working on her homework. She'd gotten a little behind in some classes and was trying to make up for it now.

"Hello?" Emma poked her head into the room. "You busy?"

Devon looked up. "Just doing homework. What's up?"

"Mom sent me over to deliver some stuff to Grandma—things for a mission project at her church. Anyway, I wanted to ask you something."

"What?" Devon set down her book.

"Well, I know you're friends with Amanda now, and that's cool. But this thing with Felicia . . . well, it's getting kinda complicated. She really is innocent and she's been the victim of bullying and—"

"Are you accusing Amanda?"

"No. Not Amanda." Emma narrowed her eyes. "Can I trust you?"

"Of course. We've been friends, like, forever. I'm living with your grandmother. Why would you not be able to trust me?"

Devon stood up and folded her arms in front. "I can't believe you'd even ask me that."

"Okay." Emma just nodded.

"So what is it?" Devon was growing more curious.

"It has to do with Tristin."

"Tristin?" This was even more interesting. Especially since Tristin considered herself to be Amanda's best friend. Something that Devon wouldn't mind seeing changed.

"I know you're friends with her too."

"Not as much as you'd think."

"How so?"

Devon considered asking Emma how much she could trust her, but knew that would sound hypocritical. "For starters, Tristin doesn't really like me all that much. I know she doesn't appreciate that I'm friends with Amanda. Or that Amanda and I are doubling up for the Christmas ball."

"Oh yeah, that makes sense."

"So what's up with Tristin? Did she bully Felicia?"

"Yes, and we have real proof." Emma told her about the saved MyPlace page. "It's not the same page that Tristin showed you, but it's got enough mean stuff on it to get Tristin into trouble at school."

"Then why not go forward with it?"

"We will. But if we could just get our hands on that really nasty page—the one Tristin showed you, the one I'm sure she made. Well, that would just blow this whole thing wide open." Emma told Devon about how Tristin was after the same guy who had been befriending Felicia. "Coincidence?"

"Interesting . . ."

"Remember how we used to play detectives when were little?" Emma asked.

Devon laughed. "Yeah. I'd always make you play Watson to my Sherlock."

"Right. Well, I wondered if you could get your hands on Tristin's iPhone or iPad or whatever she's using. And do a quick check for that page and if you find it, send it out so we can download it."

"Yeah, and while I'm at it I might discover the cure for cancer too." Devon rolled her eyes. "Emma, do you think I can just nab Tristin's phone out of her purse and do all that?"

Emma leaned forward and looked intently at Devon. "I think that if anyone can do it, you can."

"You're nuts."

"You won't even try?"

Devon pressed her lips together. "I didn't say that."

"So you will?" Emma looked hopeful.

"If I see a safe opportunity—which I seriously doubt will happen—I'll do what I can. Okay?"

Emma threw her arms around Devon, giving her a tight hug. "Thanks, Devon. I knew you'd want to help. You try to act so tough sometimes, but you've got a good heart. I knew it."

Devon tried not to act too surprised. "Well, I won't promise you anything."

"I know." Emma jingled the car keys. "I better go. I promised to come right back. Mom doesn't usually let me drive at night."

After Emma left, Devon wondered what she had promised— what she could be getting herself into. But she'd said if there was an opportunity . . . What were the chances of that?

• • • • •

The next day, Devon tried not to think too much about her promise to Emma. It wasn't that she wanted to let Emma down, but she just didn't think it was possible. Even in the locker room after conditioning, when she thought she might get a chance to sneak Tristin's phone out of her bag, it was impossible. But Devon liked a challenge. She decided to try another venue.

"I was on MyPlace last night." She said this casually to Amanda, almost confidentially, although she knew Tristin was listening. "I got to thinking about creating a new page . . ." She lowered her voice. "Not about me, but about someone else."

"Who?" Tristin asked with interest.

"No one you know," Devon said dismissively, turning her attention back to Amanda. "Anyway, I know your dad's a lawyer and I wondered if what I wanted to do was legal or not."

"What do you want to do?" Amanda stopped brushing her hair, peering curiously at Devon.

"There's this girl from my old school—a total witch. Anyway, I happened to see a nasty post on her page last night. She's so mean. I got to thinking, now that I'm not in the same school as her and no one would suspect me, it might be fun to create a MyPlace page on her. Something that would show her true colors to everyone she's been picking on. I wouldn't want to do anything that would get me into real trouble, though, you know?" Devon paused, glancing around as if she was truly worried. "I wouldn't want to cross any lines."

"Then you should just leave the whole thing alone." Amanda tossed her brush into her bag. "That's what my dad would tell you too, Devon. Don't even go there."

"Okay." Devon nodded eagerly. Mostly she wanted to remain agreeable to Amanda. "I definitely won't do it then." As she buttoned her top, she tossed a quick glance at Tristin. Unless Devon was mistaken, Tristin was studying her closely.

"I don't know why anyone would take chances like that," Amanda said as she went over to the mirror to check her makeup.

"Bad idea. I get it," Devon said. Normally, Devon would follow Amanda over there, touching up her own makeup beside her. Instead she decided to take her time, slowly folding her workout clothes, neatly placing them into the basket and fiddling with the zipper on her bag as if it wasn't working right.

"You can do it without getting caught," Tristin said quietly as she shoved her workout clothes into her own basket.

"What?" Devon acted oblivious.

"Create a page."

Devon wrinkled her nose as she reached for her bag. "Like Amanda said. Bad idea."

Tristin shrugged. "Yeah, maybe. Even if the girl is a witch . . ."

Devon acted like Tristin had struck a real chord there. "She really is. In fact, this girl's one of the reasons I came here. She was so horrid to me. And it sounds like she still is that way."

"Then get her back."

Devon glanced over to where Amanda was putting on mascara. "What about what Amanda said? Her dad's a lawyer. I don't want to get in trouble. I'm not even very good at managing my own MyPlace page. Really, I should just forget it. Stupid idea."

"What're you two jabbering about?" Amanda called out cheerfully.

"Nothing." Devon grabbed up her bag and went over to join Amanda. She felt like she had hooked Tristin and was slowly reeling her in. It felt good! But to make it work, she'd have to play it just right. She'd have to make Tristin trust her, let her think she was helping her. Her last class of the day was drama and Tristin was in it. That would be her big chance. Hopefully, Devon wouldn't have to lift a finger.

Sure enough, Tristin came straight to her as soon as Devon got to drama class in the auditorium. First Tristin made small talk since others were around to hear, but when it was just the two of them, Tristin lowered her voice. "Want me to help you?" she offered.

"Huh?" Again Devon played stupid.

"You know, to make a MyPlace page on that mean girl."

"Oh, I don't know. After what Amanda said—"

"Amanda doesn't know *everything*."

"Yeah, but I really don't want to get in trouble."

"You won't." Tristin shrugged. "But fine . . . if you're scared."

Devon stood up straighter. "You don't know me very well. I don't scare easily."

After they took their turns onstage, they arranged to meet together in the back of the auditorium where they would pretend to practice their lines. Instead, Tristin explained to Devon how it was done. She took her step by step, explaining how to use Photoshop and everything. For some reason she seemed very eager to have Devon do this. Perhaps it was a setup.

"But I don't really know how to use Photoshop," Devon told her.

"I do," Tristin said. "You can ride home with me and I'll help you do it. We'll get it up tonight if you want."

"Really?" Suddenly Devon felt even more worried. Besides the possibility that Tristin was setting Devon up, which seemed more than likely, Devon realized that Tristin would expect her to have an actual person—a high school girl with an actual MyPlace page that they could nab photos from. Who could she use? If she did use someone, would she be able to get it off in time to avoid real trouble? Maybe she was in over her head. And yet, it felt like the adventure was on. How was she going to back down? Still, she would need to proceed carefully—and without trusting Tristin.

Emma was just putting a frozen casserole into the oven when she heard the landline phone ring. Thinking it was Mom checking on her to see if she'd remembered to start dinner, she casually answered it. But to her surprise it was Devon. She sounded upset and out of breath and strange.

"What's wrong?" Emma demanded.

"Don't you ever answer your cell?" Devon shot back in a raspy voice.

"What are you talk—"

"Never mind. I *need* your help."

"What's going on?"

"I can't tell you right now, but I was trying to clear Felicia's name. Now I'm in big trouble."

"What do—"

"I'm stuck in Lakewood, trying to hide from Tristin."

"*What?*"

"I need a ride, Emma. Can you come?"

118

"Mom's not home—I have no car." Emma turned the oven to automatic timed cook. "Why are you hiding from Tristin?"

"Because she's going to *kill me*!"

"Seriously?" She ran to her bag, extracting her phone.

"Seriously! I downloaded a flash drive from her computer. She caught me and I had to run—"

"Where exactly are you?" Emma had her cell phone in the other hand now, hitting speed dial. "I'm calling Cass—maybe she can help."

Devon gave her the street coordinates. "I'm hiding in a hedge," she whispered. "I hear someone coming."

Keeping Devon on the landline phone, Emma told Cassidy it was an emergency, quickly explaining Devon's dilemma in Lakewood. "She's got the goods on Tristin. For Felicia. But she needs a ride."

"I'll pick you up first since you're on the way," Cassidy told Emma.

"We'll be there soon," Emma said into the landline, but when Devon didn't respond, Emma realized she'd already hung up. Feeling seriously concerned, Emma scrawled a quick note for Mom then grabbed her jacket and went outside to wait for Cass. It was dark and foggy and getting colder by the minute. She was tempted to call Devon to make sure she was okay, but if her phone wasn't on silent mode, it might give her away to Tristin.

Feeling like a spy in a movie, Emma stomped her feet to get warm and ran out as soon as Cassidy's car pulled up. "Devon hung up on me," she said as she jumped into the car. "It sounded like Tristin was nearby."

"This is crazy," Cassidy said as she drove away.

"I know. But Devon sounds really upset. Like she's really scared."

"What does she think Tristin will do to her?" Cassidy asked.

"She said Tristin was going to kill her."

"Seriously? *Kill* her?" Cassidy sounded doubtful as she turned onto a main road.

"I'm sure Devon's just being melodramatic, but I'm just as sure that Tristin must be furious. What kind of measures do you think she'd take to get that flash drive back?"

"I have no idea. But if Devon really got the evidence, Tristin's going to be in big trouble at school. Maybe even legal trouble."

"Tristin isn't exactly a passive sort of person. Plus she's tall." Emma cringed to think of Devon being cornered by an enraged Tristin. Who knew what she might do?

"Do you think Tristin was armed?" Cassidy sounded even more concerned now. "Is it possible her dad might have a gun or anything like that?"

"A gun?" Emma couldn't imagine Tristin with a firearm . . . or even a knife. "I don't think so. Devon didn't say anything to suggest that. But she did sound totally scared. I'm guessing Tristin is pretty desperate to get that drive back."

"This is creeping me out big-time," Cassidy said as she turned on the street that paralleled the Lakewood development. "Think we should call the police?"

"I don't know . . . I mean, really, could it be *that* serious?" Just the same, Emma reached for her phone. "Devon didn't say to call the police."

"What if we find them and Tristin is beating up Devon? Or what if she has a knife or a gun or something dangerous?"

"Oh, Cassidy, you don't think that could happen, do you?" Emma nervously fingered her phone.

"I don't know . . . but no, not really."

Emma leaned forward, peering out into the foggy darkness. "Devon said she was near the corner of Aspen and Willow." She pointed to a sign. "That's Willow, you better turn there."

"Which way?"

"I don't know." Emma looked up and down the darkened street. "Try right. If we don't find Aspen soon, we'll double back."

"This really is creepy," Cassidy said as she slowly drove down Willow. "Like I'm expecting to see Devon's lifeless, bleeding body in the middle of the street."

"Cassidy!" Emma scolded. "Now you're creeping me out."

"Why did Devon do this—go there all by herself? She should've given us a heads-up or something."

"I don't know any details." Emma was looking back and forth, trying to spot some kind of movement in the headlights.

"Maybe you should have your phone ready to call 911 . . . just in case."

"Don't worry, I do."

After slowly cruising several blocks, Emma spotted the Aspen sign. "This is the right corner!" she exclaimed. "Devon should be near here."

"Should I stop driving?" Cassidy asked. "You want to open your window and call out for her?"

"What if Tristin is nearby?" Emma cringed.

"Yeah, good point."

"Devon knows your car. She knows we're coming." Emma looked down at her phone, wondering if she should call Devon to let her know—

"Look!" Cassidy pointed to a shadowy figure on the other side of the street.

"That's Tristin," Emma whispered. "Keep driving. Don't even look at her. Just keep going."

"Where is Devon?" Cassidy asked in a hushed tone.

"She can't be far from here." Emma looked from side to side.

"Dear God," Cassidy prayed out loud. "Please, help us find Devon. Safely. Amen!"

"Amen," Emma agreed.

"Why don't you call her?" Cassidy urged. "Find out where she's hiding."

"What about the ring tone? If Tristin's nearby she'll hear it."

"Where is she?" Cassidy muttered as she slowly cruised. They were several blocks beyond where they'd spotted Tristin. "Maybe you should double back," Emma suggested. "She might still be hiding at that intersection."

As Cassidy turned back, Emma hit speed dial. "I'm calling her," she said quietly, pressing the phone to her ear to hear better.

"Hurry back!" Devon hissed as a greeting. "Same place. I saw you just now." Before Emma could warn that Tristin was nearby, Devon hung up.

"She's still at Aspen and Willow!" Emma told Cassidy. "Hurry!"

"She's not the only one there," Cassidy pointed to someone standing next to a tree alongside a driveway as they came up to the intersection. "Tristin's there too. Like she's waiting."

"I'm unlocking the doors," Emma said. "In case Devon makes a break for it."

"Just be sure to lock them back up after she's in," Cassidy commanded.

"There she is!" Emma exclaimed. Devon was making a mad dash for the car and Tristin wasn't far behind.

"Drive!" Devon yelled as she leaped into the backseat. "Go!"

Tristin pounded on the back of the car, yelling, and Cassidy stepped on the gas. The car lunged forward as Devon slammed the door and Emma pushed the lock button. "Go-go-go!" Emma screamed in terror. "Tristin looks furious!"

"Does she have a gun?" Cassidy asked as she continued driving fast.

"No," Devon said breathlessly. "But if she'd gotten her hands on me, she wouldn't have needed one."

"Are you crazy?" Emma turned around to peer at Devon. "Going to Tristin's alone like that?"

"How did you do it?" Cassidy demanded. "Tell us everything."

"I hooked Tristin earlier today," Devon explained in a gruff-sounding voice. "Got her interested in talking about MyPlace and how it wasn't that hard to create a phony page. She invited me to come home with her so she could show me her tricks." Devon coughed.

"Are you sick?" Emma asked. "Your voice sounds raspy."

"I pretended to have this bad cough while we were on her computer. I coughed so long and so hard that I convinced her to go get me some hot water and honey for my throat." She coughed again. "I could actually use some now. Anyway, it was while she was gone that I did a quick search in her photo file and found some Felicia pics. So I pulled out my flash drive and had just loaded a couple when Tristin came back."

"Oh no." Emma gasped.

"She didn't know what I'd done at first. I got up from the computer and met her at the door, but then she saw one of the pics still open on her computer and she got suspicious." Devon made a nervous laugh. "Then I did something pretty stupid, but it worked."

"What?" Cassidy and Emma asked simultaneously.

"I bumped her arm, spilling the hot water down her front as I made a break for the door. You should've heard her screaming at me."

"Was anyone home?" Cassidy asked. "Her parents?"

"Unfortunately, we were alone. So I knew I had to get out of there before she really did try to kill me. You should've heard the language she was using. And I thought Northwood girls had class." Devon laughed. "Hey, I need you to take me to Emma's grandma's house, Cass. Remember, I live there now."

Cassidy nodded, turning down the next street.

"Does Tristin know you live there?" Emma asked fearfully. "What if she comes looking for you and Grandma is—"

"Tristin doesn't know where I live," Devon assured her. "If she tries to look it up, she'll get my mom's address. If she goes looking for me there, she'll probably meet Rodney, and he can scare anyone."

"Just the same, you better call your mom and warn her," Emma said. "Tell Lisa not to give Tristin my grandma's address."

"Yeah. Good point." As Cassidy drove, Devon called her mom and without going into details explained that a crazy girl was looking for her. "Do not tell her where I'm staying," Devon commanded. "This girl is totally psycho. I'm not kidding, Mom. In fact, if she shows up, you might want to call the police. Seriously!"

Devon was just hanging up with her mom when they got to Emma's grandma's house. "Thanks for rescuing me," she said lightly. "I'll fill you in on the rest of it tomorrow."

"So we can schedule a meeting with Mrs. Dorman in the morning?" Emma asked eagerly. "And present all our evidence to clear Felicia's name?"

"Sure." Devon grinned. "See you tomorrow."

"Wow." Cassidy shook her head as they watched Devon running up to the house. "That was a little too much excitement for one night."

"I think Devon thrives on excitement." Emma let out a long sigh. "At least she's got the goods on Tristin. I can't wait to tell Felicia."

"Should she come to our meeting tomorrow?" Cassidy asked as she backed out.

"Maybe it would be easier on Felicia not to be there," Emma said. "It seems cruel to make her sit there and see the evidence all over again. Pretty demeaning, you know."

"Right."

Before long they were back at Emma's. "Thanks for being willing to run out there like that," Emma told Cassidy. "I don't know what we would've done without you."

"It was worth it," Cassidy assured her. "To help Felicia."

"I'll tell her how you helped," Emma promised as she opened the door. "I'm sure she'll appreciate it. I plan to call her as soon as I get inside."

Emma was slightly relieved to see that Mom wasn't home yet. As she went inside, she realized that she hadn't even been gone for an hour so the casserole wasn't finished cooking yet. She dialed Felicia's number and, after apologizing for calling at dinnertime, told her the good news.

Felicia let out a happy squeal. "That's so wonderful! Thank you so much, Emma. I can't wait to tell my parents I get to return to Northwood."

"Well, we won't know for sure until tomorrow, but I don't see any reason they can keep you out. If anything, they owe you an apology."

"Tristin is the one who owes me an apology."

"That's for sure. You should've seen how angry she was. Devon was really brave to do that for you."

"I owe Devon my life."

"Cassidy drove the getaway car. You should've seen her go."

"I owe her too."

"So we'll let you know how it all shakes down tomorrow. After we meet with Mrs. Dorman, I'll call you. Okay?"

"Thank you so much, Emma. I really do owe you. Big-time!"

"We're just glad to see you're going to be treated fairly. *Finally.*" After Emma hung up, she went back to working on the Santa sleigh. So far she'd cut the box into a graceful sleighlike shape. Spotting an old pair of roller skates in the garage, she chopped off the tops of them and, using hot glue, adhered the wheel portions to the bottom of the sleigh—making it appear as if the sleigh was gliding along. Then she painted the whole thing hot pink. She'd considered going with a traditional Christmas red, but thought it might be more interesting to make this sleigh flashy and colorful. As she left it in the garage to dry, she felt a real sense of accomplishment. Not because of the sleigh so much but because of how things were looking up for Felicia. And, she decided as she went into the house, petite Felicia was just the right size to play the second elf with Emma at Friday's promotional assembly. After all, hadn't she just said that she owed Emma big-time? Emma had no problem letting her pay up by being an elf.

As she dipped a spoon into her yogurt container, Bryn tried to hide her exasperation at her bickering friends. So much for eating lunch in peace. First Amanda and Tristin got all weird on her, just because Bryn didn't want to eat with them at their table. Maybe that was a mistake. Especially since it felt like the DG was having a total meltdown today. Why couldn't people just get along?

"What's wrong with her?" Emma demanded as she waved her cell in the air. "She won't answer my texts or her phone."

"Maybe Devon doesn't want to talk to you," Bryn said with nonchalance.

"She ignored my texts too," Cassidy pointed out.

"Maybe she doesn't want to talk to either of you." Bryn winked at Abby, who simply rolled her eyes. Abby was still in a snit because she thought Bryn wasn't doing her fair share of her work on Project Santa Sleigh. She'd actually accused Bryn of only wanting the limelight. Never mind that Bryn and Jason had gotten a huge donation to ensure that the dance benefit could become a reality.

"Right," Emma snapped at Bryn. "I suppose Devon would talk to you?"

Bryn pulled out her phone. "Maybe she would." She called Devon's cell phone and to her surprise, Devon answered.

"Hey, Devon," Bryn said smoothly. "What's up? Are you sick or something?"

"Yeah." Devon coughed loudly. "Laryngitis."

"Oh, that's too bad. Cass and Em thought maybe you'd died or something. They've been trying to reach you." Bryn wrinkled her nose at her friends. It was obvious that Cass and Em were not amused.

"I want to talk to her," Emma declared.

"Em wants to talk to you," Bryn informed Devon.

"I'm not supposed to talk," Devon said hoarsely.

"Oh." Bryn tipped her head to Em. "She's not supposed to talk. Laryngitis."

"Then tell her she can listen." Emma was reaching for the phone.

"Emma says you can listen." Bryn extended the phone and Emma grabbed it.

"Devon," she said sternly. "What's going on? Cassidy and I set up the appointment with Mrs. Dorman. It's not until after school. But you're not here." Emma scowled as she listened. "Okay, fine. You're sick. So you can just send the pictures and we'll show them to—" Emma stopped talking, but as she listened her blue eyes grew bigger. "What?" she shrieked. "You can't be serious. Where did you lose it?" She exchanged a worried look with Cassidy now. "Have you looked everywhere? Checked all your pockets? Do you think it's in Cassidy's car?"

"What is it?" Cassidy asked.

128

"She lost the flash drive."

"No way." Cassidy threw her head back and groaned.

"Maybe it's where you were hiding last night. Cass and I could run over there after school and look for it." She shook her head grimly. "I can't believe you lost it, Devon. That's going to ruin everything . . . No, I'm not blaming you. Well, not exactly. Are you sure it's not in the house somewhere?" Emma let out a hopeless little sigh, told Devon good-bye, and handed Bryn back her phone.

"Bad news, huh?" Bryn slipped her phone back into her bag.

"The worst."

"Maybe she lost it in my car." Cassidy took a bite of her apple. "I'll go look as soon as I finish my lunch."

"I'll help you," Emma offered.

"So what does this mean for Felicia?" Abby asked with concern.

"Good question." Emma wadded up a napkin.

"We're not giving up," Cassidy said as she chewed. "I've got a really good defense planned for Felicia. With or without Devon's contribution."

"I can't believe that after all we went through last night, Devon actually lost the drive." Emma was already gathering her stuff. "Come on, Cass. Let's go see if it's in the backseat of your car."

"We'll be right back," Cass told them. "Hopefully with the drive."

After Emma and Cassidy were gone, it was just Bryn and Abby. And it was plain to see that Abby was still a little out of sorts. She was folding a napkin into tiny triangles over and over—a sign that she was frustrated.

"You're mad at me, aren't you?" Bryn asked.

Abby shrugged. "I don't think I'd use the word mad."

"Perturbed? Aggravated? Irritated?" Bryn made a half smile. "Do any of those fit?"

"Maybe." Abby pursed her lips. "It's just that we're supposed to be partnering on Project Santa Sleigh, right?"

"Right."

"I'm in charge of the whole project. Plus it feels like I'm going to be responsible for our own sleigh project too. Do you really think that's fair?"

"I never said you were in charge of our own sleigh project," Bryn clarified. "I simply said that I haven't had time to do anything."

"And that means what?"

"It means I've got a lot on my plate right now."

Abby looked unconvinced. Now she actually seemed mad.

"Look, Abby." Bryn softened her tone. "I'm willing to do more. But you act like I've been doing nothing. Already I've helped to secure the funds for the dance. As well as the prizes, which are pretty fabulous if I do say so. Besides that, I've gotten everything all set up for Friday's assembly, in which I will be starring—"

"Starring?" Abby blinked. "Really? That's how you see yourself? Like you're the star of the show?"

"Sorry . . . for lack of another word."

"Oh, I think it was rather fitting," Abby said a bit smugly. "Bryn Jacobs, the star of Project Santa Sleigh. Never mind that she sloughs off the work on all her friends while she goes out getting her hair and nails done."

"Seriously?" Bryn frowned. "That's how you think of me?"

"Well, you did admit that you have an appointment this week."

"Yes . . . something I do about once a month. Nothing new about that. Besides, you seem to forget that I'm also supervising both dance committees—the one for the actual dance as well as the benefit. What more do you want me to do?"

"For starters, you could help me build our sleigh," Abby said in a snippy tone. "That shouldn't be all up to me alone."

"What about letting the boys handle that part of the project?" Bryn suggested. "Why is it that all the girls seem to assume it's their responsibility? Guys do know how to wield a knife to cut cardboard, don't they? Or how to apply some paint?"

Abby seemed to consider this. "Okay, that's probably a good point. Hopefully, we'll get our dates lined up after the assembly."

"Yeah. That was the plan, remember?" Bryn felt somewhat vindicated.

"Right. So I won't obsess over the sleigh anymore. I guess I was getting worried because of what Emma was saying. Don't forget—this is a competition. Just because we're on the committees doesn't mean we can't win, right?"

"No, we never said that, but we do need to ensure that the judges are impartial." Bryn was making a mental note to herself about this. "And everyone needs to know that's the situation."

"Anyway, it sounds like Emma and Cass's sleigh is already coming along nicely. I guess I was feeling a little jealous."

"That's because Emma's an artist. FYI, it sounds like Emma's been doing all the work herself. Don't forget that their sleigh had to get done early so she can bring it to the assembly as our sample. Remember?" Bryn wanted to point out that Abby was acting pretty childish but knew that wouldn't help matters.

Abby made a slight nod. "Yeah, you're right. I remember." Even so she was still frowning. "But . . ."

"But . . . you're still ticked at me, aren't you? Did I do something else to offend you, Abs?" Bryn's patience was wearing thinner.

Abby glanced over to the table where Amanda and Tristin

were sitting with their usual friends. "Lately I get the feeling you'd rather be with them," she said slowly, "than here with your old friends."

Bryn held up her hands. "Hey, can you blame me? Cass and Em were going on and on about Devon. You were acting put out. The tension here was getting a little old."

"That's nothing new. We don't always get along, but we're usually loyal to each other. Besides, it's not like Amanda and Tristin are candidates for Miss Congeniality."

"They look pretty congenial to me." Bryn wished she could entice Abby to go with her over there to join Amanda and her friends. That might help change her attitude toward them.

"What about what Cass and Em said about Tristin? That she's the one responsible for what happened to Felicia? Doesn't that bother you at all?" Abby's tone sounded very accusing.

"We don't know that for certain, Abs. Cass and Em admitted they never saw a shred of evidence. Now Devon claims she's lost it anyway. Seems pretty flimsy if you ask me." Bryn looked over to where Amanda and Tristin were laughing with their friends—having fun instead of casting suspicion on others. "Really, I cannot imagine that Tristin would do something that despicable."

"Or that Amanda would be involved?" Abby tilted her head to one side.

"I seriously doubt Amanda would do something that low-down and lame. The more I think about it, the more ridiculous it seems. And that whole story about Devon and the flash drive . . . *really?*"

"I don't know about that." Abby's brow creased. "I do know that having Amanda in the DG makes everything feel different."

"Are you blaming me for that too? I mean, sure, I like Amanda, but I wasn't the one who invited her into the DG. You can blame Devon for that."

"It was originally your idea, Bryn. You can't deny that. And you and Amanda obviously get along just fine."

"I try to get along with *everyone* . . . or haven't you noticed?" Bryn gave her a tolerant smile.

"Yeah. I get that. But when Amanda mentioned the possibility of Tristin joining the DG—followed by Cass and Em's little fireworks show—well, it's like the DG is changing. And not for the better."

"What's not for the better?" Cassidy sat next to Bryn.

"Nothing," Abby mumbled.

Bryn peered curiously at Emma and Cassidy. "Any luck?"

"No." Emma glumly shook her head.

"What's going on?" Cassidy asked. "Looks like you guys are having another disagreement. What about the DG is changing for the worse?"

"Abby's all worked up over Amanda and Tristin," Bryn said lightly.

"Well, Abby's not the only one," Emma declared. "No way will I ever agree that Tristin can join the DG. If she's in, I'm out."

"Same goes for me," Cassidy said. "After last night, I'm pretty certain Devon would vote no as well."

"So, really, it's a moot point." Bryn set her empty yogurt carton on the tray with a clunk.

"We weren't just discussing Tristin," Abby continued. "I was expressing my opinion on Amanda. Since she joined the DG, things are different. Not in a good way."

Emma and Cassidy exchanged looks then nodded somberly. "Yeah, we were just talking about that too," Emma admitted. "Things are changing."

"Like I just told Abs a few minutes ago, I was *not* the one to invite Amanda into the DG. And I don't plan to be the one to uninvite her either." Bryn slowly stood. "FYI, it was Devon, and she kind of jumped the gun too."

"Well, if we had that flash drive right now, like we'd expected, we would find out if Amanda had any involvement in the Felicia scandal," Cassidy told them. "If she did, we were going to request that she be ousted from the DG."

"That's right," Emma chimed in. "I'm guessing that once Felicia is in the DG, like we hope she'll be, Amanda will want to quit anyway."

"Oh, I'm sure Tristin will want to be in a club with the same girl she bullied," Cassidy said sarcastically.

"You honestly think that Tristin will still be in this school after that flash drive exposes her?" Abby asked.

Bryn waved a finger in front of their faces. "You girls are forgetting something. Right now *there is no flash drive*. As far as we know, there may never have been one. It seems like if anyone is acting questionable here, it might be Devon."

Abby looked shocked. "You'd take Amanda and Tristin's side over Devon's?"

"What about DG rule number two?" Cassidy blurted. "We're supposed to be loyal to each other."

"All I'm saying is that Amanda and Tristin have a deeper history at Northwood than Devon," Bryn pointed out. "I agree we should be loyal, but you guys know the crazy stunts Devon's pulled. Does anyone here totally trust that girl?"

"Does anyone totally trust Tristin?" Emma challenged Bryn. "Do you?"

Bryn considered this. "I'm not sure. I guess I need more evidence to make up my mind." She picked up her bag. "Evidence that seems to be missing." As she looped a strap over her shoulder, she gave them a sugary smile. "I'm sure everything will work out just fine in the end, girls. Now, as much as I hate to leave your delightful company, I must pay a visit to the ladies' room."

As Bryn strolled away, she felt completely fed up with her DG friends. Their obsession on proving Felicia's innocence seemed to be interfering with everything. Not only was it distracting them from the task at hand—the Christmas ball—it seemed to be dividing them as friends as well. Were they going to allow their concerns over Felicia to unravel the DG? Then again, who knew—maybe that would be for the best.

15

While Cassidy waited for Emma to meet her in the counseling center after school, she texted and called Devon, but without any luck. Apparently Devon was still playing hard to get.

"Sorry I'm late," Emma said as she hurried into the waiting area.

"It's okay. Someone's in there with Mrs. Dorman anyway." Cassidy held up her phone. "Do you think Devon is really sick? Or just ignoring me?"

"She's ignoring me too."

"I'm guessing that means she still hasn't found the flash drive." Cassidy scowled. "This will be an uphill battle without it."

"I know how to get her." Emma reached for her own phone. "I'll call my grandma on the landline."

Cassidy went over her notes for their meeting as Emma talked to her grandmother. When Emma hung up, Cassidy could tell that she'd gotten nowhere. "Grandma says she's sleeping, and it seems she really does have laryngitis."

"Probably from all that coughing at Tristin's." Cassidy folded the paper with her notes in half. "But Devon saw the photos on Tristin's computer. That makes her a witness. Even without the drive, we can get her in here to talk to Mrs. Dorman as soon as she's well."

Emma pointed toward Mrs. Dorman's office where the door was opening. A man and woman were thanking Mrs. Dorman, shaking her hand, and leaving. "Looks like we're next," Emma said quietly.

"Ready for this?" Cassidy whispered.

Emma just nodded and Cassidy led the way.

"Come in, girls." Mrs. Dorman smiled as she closed the door behind them. "I understand this is about Felicia Ruez."

"That's right," Cassidy began as soon as they were seated. "We have good reason to believe that Felicia was set up. She never created that MyPlace page, and she's been bullied."

Mrs. Dorman's dark brows arched. "That's quite a list. Do you have any evidence? Or is this all just speculative?"

"We have *some* evidence." Cassidy turned on her iPad. "Felicia gave me her password so I could open her email and show you the messages that were sent to her the past couple of months. It's obvious that she's been bullied." Cassidy opened an email and slid it over for Mrs. Dorman to read.

"This is very concerning." Mrs. Dorman removed her reading glasses. "But who sent it? Who's TwistiGirl?"

"Tristin Wilson." Cassidy opened another email.

"Really?" Mrs. Dorman looked shocked. "You know this for a fact?"

"It's easy to prove," Emma explained. "Even if Tristin has closed the email account, which I'm guessing she's done, it's all traceable."

Cassidy slid her iPad across the desk again. "Here's another one. Felicia saved ten or so. She dumped some of the earlier ones before she realized she should save them."

"If this really is Tristin's account, it does appear to be bullying." Mrs. Dorman peered at Cassidy and Emma. "But you also said Felicia didn't create that MyPlace page. Can you prove that too?"

"We thought we had evidence last night." Cassidy quickly told the story about Devon and the flash drive, and Mrs. Dorman looked even more shocked.

"Where is this flash drive?" she asked.

"Devon seems to have lost it," Emma said sadly.

"However, Devon did see the photos on Tristin's computer. That would make her an eyewitness." Cassidy explained about Devon's laryngitis. "I'm sure we can get her to come in and talk to you . . . when she's able to actually talk."

"Interesting . . ."

"We're certain that Tristin has destroyed the photo evidence by now," Emma added.

"If someone had just downloaded the MyPlace page." Cassidy shook her head. "That would be evidence in itself."

"Yes, that's a point that's been made by a number of people," Mrs. Dorman admitted. "A good lesson for everyone."

"Can you see how wrong this is?" Cassidy asked. "To expel Felicia when she's actually the victim here?"

"What about Felicia's recent changes in her clothing?" Mrs. Dorman said suddenly. "She faced disciplinary action for inappropriate dress. It seemed to substantiate the MyPlace page. How do you explain that?"

Both Cassidy and Emma took turns telling Mrs. Dorman about how Felicia had gotten teased for wearing childish outfits. "Her mom made her dress like that," Emma said as Cassidy pulled up another email. "It made her look like a little girl. Felicia took matters into her own hands." Emma told about how Felicia snuck what she thought were more sophisticated clothes to school. "And she dressed in the restroom."

"Oh my."

"Look at this." Cassidy slid the iPad over again. "See where Tristin is calling her Baby Girl and Chiquita Slut and a bunch of other names all related to Felicia's ethnicity as well as how she was dressed."

"This isn't just bullying. That's racist too." Mrs. Dorman grimly shook her head. "Something we want to nip in the bud. If you girls are right—if this is from a Northwood student—something will be done immediately to rectify it."

"Good." Cassidy closed her iPad. "Because I know Felicia's dad has considered hiring an attorney."

Mrs. Dorman pressed her lips together.

"We wouldn't want to see our school portrayed as racist," Cassidy said somberly. "I'm sure the media would love to make it into something more than it is."

"Has anyone spoken to the media about any of this?" Mrs. Dorman looked worried.

"Not yet."

"Well, I plan to go directly to Mr. Worthington with this new information." She looked down at the iPad. "Do you mind if I borrow this? To show him?"

"Sure." Cassidy nodded.

"We'll talk to Devon and see if she's going to be in school tomorrow," Emma told her. "So she can tell you about what she saw."

"Or maybe she's found the drive," Cassidy said hopefully.

"We might even go look around the neighborhood where it could've gotten lost," Emma said.

Mrs. Dorman stood. "You girls are being very good friends to poor Felicia. I'm sure she must appreciate it."

"It seemed the least we could do," Emma said.

"If you see Felicia, please tell her that we're working on this. Tell her that we do want the truth to come out. If she's been the victim—as it appears she has—we will do everything possible to make things right with her." Mrs. Dorman shook both their hands. "Thank you for coming forward for her like this. Tell Felicia that we'll be in touch soon. Very soon."

They were barely out of the counseling center when Emma called Felicia to tell her the good news. "Well, it's good news for the most part." Emma explained about the missing flash drive. "But we're going to look for it, and we still have Devon's eyewitness account. Mrs. Dorman said they'll take that into consideration too."

By the time Emma ended her conversation with Felicia, they were at the car. "I think we should go talk to Devon first," Cassidy said as she started the car. "Make sure she doesn't have the drive. We can look around the house too. Then, if we don't find it, we'll go back to Tristin's neighborhood and look around."

"Hopefully we won't run into Tristin."

"Speaking of Tristin . . ." Cassidy frowned. "Don't you think it's weird that she was acting totally normal today? Like nothing was wrong? You'd think she'd be a little nervous, wouldn't you?"

"You'd think. Maybe she's just playing it cool. Besides, she probably figured out early on that Devon was absent. Maybe she thinks that's buying her time, or maybe she's been covering her trail so well that she thinks she can't get caught."

Cassidy hit her fist into the steering wheel. "Or maybe she found the drive!"

"Oh no!" Emma slapped her forehead. "I'll bet you're right."

"It makes perfect sense. If Tristin found the drive, she'd be feeling pretty confident right now."

"Although she must still be seriously ticked at Devon for last night. Do you think that's why Devon is laying low today?"

"I don't know. But laryngitis or not, Devon is going to do some talking," Cassidy declared.

Because it was her grandmother's house, Emma led them inside without even knocking. "Grandma," she called out. "It's just me."

"Oh, hello dear." Emma's grandmother hugged her. "And Cassidy too. Are you girls here to see me? Or checking on Devon?"

"Both," Emma told her. "How are you?"

"Just fine. I think our patient is on the mend too."

"Good." Emma glanced down the hallway. "Can we visit her?"

"You know the way."

They discovered Devon sitting in bed, watching a movie on her laptop. "Enjoying your little vacation?" Cassidy asked.

Devon rolled her eyes and shut down the laptop. "What do you guys want?" she said in a raspy voice.

"What do you *think* we want?" Emma sat down on the bed.

"I don't have it." Devon folded her arms in front of her.

"Then we'll look around for it," Cassidy said in a friendly tone. Strolling around the room, she peeked in the closet and under the bed and into dark corners. "Being that you've been under the weather, it's possible that you dropped it in here someplace and—"

"You don't have to do that," Devon snapped.

"We want to." Emma was poking around the quilt and under the pillows.

"Knock it off," Devon complained.

"We *have* to find it," Cassidy told her. "It's the one thing that will totally clear Felicia's—"

"I *don't* have it!"

"Could you have dropped it near Tristin's house?" Cassidy asked. "Do you think she might've found it?"

Now Emma told Devon about how confident Tristin had seemed today. "Not at all like the guilty criminal who was about to be exposed."

Devon just shrugged, reaching for her laptop again.

"When was the last time you saw the flash drive?" Cassidy asked. "Did you have it when you got in the car last night?"

"I can't remember."

"When did you realize you'd lost it?" Emma asked.

"I don't recall." Devon started watching the movie again.

"What color is the drive?" Cassidy asked. "That might help us to spot it if it's on the ground."

"Purple." Devon made an exasperated sigh. "Really, if I'm going to recover my voice, I'm supposed to keep quiet. That's what Grandma Betty told me."

Cassidy looked at Emma. "Well, it's probably not here anyway. Want to go over to Lakewood and poke around?"

"Good luck if you run into Tristin," Devon growled at them.

"Get well," Cassidy told her. "You need to be able to talk because we promised Mrs. Dorman that you'd be an eyewitness and—"

"You *what*?" Devon glared at Cassidy.

"We told her you saw the photos on Tristin's computer," Emma explained. "That makes you an eyewitness, Devon. Your testimony is almost as good as the flash drive."

"Come on," Cassidy urged Emma. "Let's get going while it's still light enough to see something."

It wasn't until they were in the car that Cassidy confessed her concerns about Devon. "I feel like she's holding back on us. I mean, last night, she was all forthcoming and excited about getting that evidence. Now it's like . . . well . . . ."

"Like she doesn't care."

"Exactly."

"So aggravating."

"You know what else is aggravating?" Emma said in a slightly defeated tone. "We should be at home right now—working on our Santa sleigh. We have three days to get it done in time for Friday's assembly."

"That's true, but don't forget midterms. We really should be home studying right now." Cassidy turned into Lakewood. "Here's what we'll do, Em. I'll park right where we picked up Devon last night and we'll split up and give ourselves fifteen minutes to look around. Okay?"

"Okay. Chances are that Tristin already found it anyway."

"Probably. But for Felicia's sake we need to do this."

"And if we see Tristin?" Emma sounded worried.

"Keep your phone handy."

As it turned out they spent more like thirty minutes searching for the mysterious missing flash drive. They found a pop can, gum wrapper, tennis ball, and a little pink mitten—but no purple drive. At least they never ran into Tristin. Eventually, admitting that the light was fading, they both agreed it was a fool's errand and time to go home.

Neither of them said a word as Cassidy started the car and slowly drove out of Tristin's neighborhood. "We shouldn't feel like we failed," she finally said as she turned onto Emma's street. "After all, we had a great meeting with Mrs. Dorman this afternoon. Even without the flash drive, it seems certain that Felicia will be vindicated."

"Yeah. That's great, but I was just thinking about Devon . . . the way she reacted when you told her about needing to be an eyewitness."

"That was kinda strange."

"It makes me think about what Bryn was saying earlier, asking if we totally trusted Devon."

"You know Devon better than any of us. Do you trust her . . . completely?" Cassidy pulled into the driveway, then turned to look at Emma.

"No way. Not completely."

"Do you think she's been honest with us in regard to the situation with Felicia and wanting to help out?"

"I'm not sure. I thought so at first, but something about how she was acting this afternoon just doesn't ring true. She's holding back about something. I can't tell what it is though."

"I know." Cassidy nodded.

"Well, I better get to work."

"Sorry I can't help with the sleigh tonight, Em. I've got a ton of reading to do, but I'll try to work on it with you tomorrow—if you want."

"That's probably better anyway. I'll have everything ready by then. And I can put you to work." Emma got out and, closing the door, waved.

As Cassidy drove toward home, she still felt a keen sense of disappointment. Like things hadn't really worked out how she'd planned. She just hoped that today's faux pas wouldn't reflect badly on Felicia. Mrs. Dorman seemed relatively convinced of Felicia's evidence—what little there was of it. But would there be enough to clearly indict Tristin? Or was it possible that, like Bryn seemed to believe, Tristin wasn't even involved? As Cassidy parked in front of her house, she realized that her best solution to all of this was probably to just pray. Let God sort it out.

Devon had felt on top of the world last night. As she'd hurried up to her room with her magnificent flash drive in hand, she'd decided she should go into some form of espionage as a career. As she downloaded the files into her laptop, she imagined herself as a chic elegant spy (aka Jane Bond) worming state secrets from unsuspecting diabolical characters and having a good time doing it. But before the drive was completely downloaded, she noticed that her phone had a new text message from Tristin.

Answer your phone or suffer the consequences.

Devon texted back: *What consequences?*

I'll tell everyone what you did to Jessica Burns.

Okay, this was a little concerning. Jessica Burns was the girl that Devon had pretended to want to make the fake MyPlace page for. In reality, Jessica had been a serious pain in the rear for Devon and, if anyone deserved to be trashed through social networking, it was Jessica. But even so, Devon had never planned to launch that page.

Devon texted again: *I didn't do anything. Don't know what you mean.* Devon was no fool. She knew that texts were like any other form of technology—they could be used against you.

Answer your phone, or I'll tell everyone what you did. I mean it.

Devon stared at the threat, wondering if it was something she could use against Tristin. But Tristin was being very careful. So far everything she'd written sounded more incriminating to Devon than to Tristin. So she just waited, and when her phone chimed, she answered.

"What's up?" she asked innocently.

"Your MyPlace page for Jessica Burns," Tristin answered nonchalantly.

"Huh?" Devon felt a rush of panic. Tristin had actually posted the page?

"That's right. The page *you* made on Jessica is up and running. Check it out if you want."

"The page *I* made?" Devon glanced at her laptop. The Felicia pics were downloaded, but she wasn't online yet. She clicked to connect.

"Yes. Remember, while I was teaching you how to do it, we did most of the photo work on your laptop. Very convenient."

"Yeah, but—"

"Check it out."

Seeing she was online, Devon went to MyPlace. "What name did you give her?"

"Me?" Tristin laughed. "You're the creator, Devon. Don't you remember?" Now Tristin told Devon what sounded like a very skanky name.

Devon typed in the words and—presto—Jessica's altered photos popped up. Along with some jargon that was very insinuating. "Why did you do this?" Devon demanded.

"Moi?"

Devon stared at the page in horror. "Tristin, you are evil."

"But this is your page," Tristin said lightly. "And I'm about to contact a friend of mine who will give it a boost. Then it will go viral and—"

"Don't you dare!"

"Not me, Devon. I'm not that stupid. This is *your* work. It all tracks back to you and your computer. When poor Jessica Burns finds out, she'll come looking for you. She'll probably bring the law with her." Tristin laughed.

"Why are you doing this?" Devon asked helplessly.

"Because of what you did to me." Tristin's voice grew more menacing. "You share those photos you stole with anyone, and I will make sure that you're blamed for Jessica's MyPlace page."

"Blackmail?"

"Call it what you like. If I go down, you go down with me." Then she hung up.

Devon went right back to the MyPlace page, determined to get it removed ASAP. Because she wasn't all that techie, she tried all sorts of things and was not having a bit of luck. The more she tried, the more impossible it became. Finally, MyPlace knocked her off their site, and she found a message from them in her email announcing that she was temporarily banned from using their social network altogether.

Devon decided to do damage control of a different kind. She had no doubt that Tristin would try to use this situation to alienate her from Amanda, but she was shocked at how quickly it all went down. Before she'd joined Grandma Betty for dinner, she'd sent Amanda several texts. All of which Amanda ignored. Then after dinner and helping with cleanup, Devon attempted to call Amanda. No answer. Finally, after Devon finished some homework and was about to get ready for bed, she noticed that Amanda had sent a text. Eager to connect with a friend, she opened it.

Leave me alone. Tristin told me what you did. I saw it on MyPlace for myself. I'm blocking you. From my phone and from my life.

Devon considered texting back but realized it was probably useless. Amanda had warned her not to get involved in something like this from the get-go. With the spin that Tristin had probably given it, Devon would look like an evil idiot. How could everything have gone sideways like this—and in just a few hours? Of course, she knew the answer to that—she had let her guard down around a girl like Tristin. What a fool!

After a sleepless night, she had gotten up with a sore throat and a hoarse voice and decided to feign a bad case of laryngitis. Sweet Grandma Betty had been very sympathetic, insisting Devon should stay home and rest her vocal chords and drink chamomile tea. Of course, Devon knew that she was only postponing the inevitable. But why not enjoy some downtime while she was at it? Of course, her downtime was interrupted numerous times by all the text messages and phone calls her "friends" in the DG were making. It wasn't until she was dumb enough to answer Bryn's call that she was forced to lie. She did not feel the least bit good about it, but really, what could she do?

Just when she'd lost herself in a good chick flick, Cass and Em showed up. All full of energy and enthusiasm, they were determined to ransack her bedroom in search of the missing flash drive. Naturally, Devon had not been cooperative. The truth was she'd simply wanted to dig a hole and crawl into it. She knew she'd let her friends down and she hated herself for continuing to deceive them. At least her lies had gotten them out of her hair temporarily. However, she knew she wouldn't be able to hold them off for long. She also knew that Grandma Betty expected her to go to school in the morning.

As Devon was printing out a book report that was due this week, she made a decision. She was going to come clean. First with her friends. Then with Mrs. Dorman in regard to Felicia. After that . . . well, she'd tell the truth and she'd accept the consequences. As she got ready for bed, she wondered if she would end up in juvie hall. That's something her mom used to threaten her with. It might not be that bad. The worst thing, she thought as she climbed into bed, would be the look on Grandma Betty's face. Just tonight, as Devon was helping to clean up the dinner dishes, Grandma Betty had made a sweet little speech.

"You are going to be something very special someday, Devon. I can just feel it in my bones. God has some very big plans for you. I'm so grateful I've been able to play a small part in it." Then she'd hugged her.

Naturally, Devon had been speechless. She'd simply thanked Grandma Betty, then insisted on finishing up the kitchen chores on her own. "Go put your feet up," she'd told her.

Now as Devon lay in bed, she wished she'd taken the time to tell Grandma Betty about the mess she'd gotten herself into this week. After opening up her home and her heart, didn't Grandma Betty deserve that much? So Devon got out of bed and tiptoed down the hall, but seeing no strip of light under Grandma Betty's door, she tiptoed back to her room.

As she got back into bed, she remembered how often Grandma Betty had assured Devon that no problem was too big for God. She'd told Devon again and again that she could go to God and tell him anything and that he would answer. Devon decided to give it a try. After years of avoiding God, it still felt a little strange to go running to him just because she was in trouble.

"Dear God," she whispered in the darkness. "I know I don't talk to you real regularly—I haven't since I was a little girl. But I want to get back into the habit. Anyway, I realize I've made some big messes in my life. Sometimes my whole life just seems like one great big mess. Somehow I always manage to slip out of them. But I think the mess I made this week might be the one that gets me. The crazy thing is that I was actually trying to help someone this time. Does that make any difference to you? Anyway, I'd really like to keep going to school at Northwood. I'd like to keep my friends in the DG. I'd like to be able to continue living here at Grandma Betty's too. But I know I need to tell the truth tomorrow. I need to help clear Felicia's name. Please, help me out of this mess. Amen."

●●●●●

After a surprisingly good night's sleep, Devon got up early in the morning. The first thing she did was text Em and Cass, saying that she needed to talk to them before school. Cass texted back, offering to give Devon a ride. Next, Devon sat down at the breakfast table with Grandma Betty, explaining about what she'd done in regard to the MyPlace page and Jessica Burns. "I never intended for it to really go out," she told her. "It was only to vindicate Felicia. But it all kinda backfired on me."

It took some time and convincing for Grandma Betty to grasp the seriousness of Devon's situation. "It might even be illegal," Devon confessed. "I'm not totally sure about that. But I do know that it's enough to get me expelled from school. I plan to tell the truth first thing when I get to school. So you never know . . ."

Grandma Betty came over and put her arms around Devon. "I'm going to be praying for you this morning. I'm going to pray that God brings goodness out of what seems bad. He can do it."

Devon brightened a little. "I prayed last night," she said quietly. "It still feels a little awkward to go running to God—I mean after all the years I spent avoiding him. But it feels pretty good too."

Grandma Betty patted Devon's back. "This is just the beginning of something good. I know it. I have confidence in God, and I have confidence in you."

Devon didn't feel the least bit confident as she climbed into the backseat of Cassidy's car. "I have the flash drive," she immediately told them. "I'm going to turn it over to Mrs. Dorman this morning. But first I have to tell you guys the truth."

"The truth about what?" Emma asked.

"I did something pretty stupid to get those photos off of Tristin's computer," she admitted. She told them the whole sordid tale.

"You made a MyPlace page smearing someone else?" Cassidy asked in a horrified tone.

"Like you thought two wrongs made a right?" Emma added.

"I know. I already told you guys, it was stupid. Really, really stupid, okay?"

"No kidding." Cassidy slowly shook her head as she turned into the school parking lot.

"Why did you trust Tristin in the first place?" Emma demanded. "We told you how she'd bullied Felicia and you knew she'd done the MyPlace page on her. You should've known she could pull something like this."

"I thought I was smarter than her," Devon confessed.

"And look where that got you." Cassidy pulled into a parking space.

No one said a word as they got out of the car and trudged through the cold, damp fog toward the school. Devon felt like she was on her way to the executioners. She was a bit dismayed that her friends hadn't been just slightly more sympathetic.

"Well, I just wanted you guys to know." Devon pulled open the front door to the school. "Before the cops show up and haul me away."

"Oh, that's not going to happen." Emma frowned at her. "Is it?"

"I don't know." Devon took in a deep breath. "Anyway, here goes."

"Wait." Cassidy put a hand on Devon's shoulder. "Want us to come with you?"

"Why?" Devon was afraid to feel hopeful.

"So we can back up your story," Cassidy told her.

"Yeah," Emma agreed. "We'll tell Mrs. Dorman that you really did what you did because you wanted to help Felicia."

"Because we asked for your help," Cassidy added.

"And that you never meant it to become a MyPlace page."

"You guys will do that?"

"Yeah." Cassidy linked arms with her. "Let's go."

After a short, nerve-wracking wait, the three girls were admitted into Mrs. Dorman's office, and without hesitating, Devon handed over the flash drive and started to confess.

"Wait a minute, wait a minute." Mrs. Dorman held up both hands. "Am I getting this right? You are telling me that you are guilty of doing the exact same thing that you're accusing Tristin of doing?"

"Not on purpose."

"You accidentally created a slanderous MyPlace page on a girl that you admit you can't stand?" Mrs. Dorman was taking notes on a yellow legal pad.

"I know it sounds unbelievable, but I never meant for it to go up. Tristin is the one who put it up. I wasn't even there."

"But you say that some of the material on the page originated on your computer?" She wrote this down too.

"Yes, but that's because Tristin insisted I use my own laptop. She said that was the only way she could teach me. I went along because I needed to win her trust. I knew I'd have to get her to leave me alone in her room long enough to get this." Devon picked up the purple flash drive.

"This is going to turn into your word against Tristin's." Mrs. Dorman looked up from her notes with a doubtful expression.

"Look," Devon said. "Why do you think I came in here and confessed to you?"

Mrs. Dorman frowned. "I'm not sure."

Devon held out the drive. "I wanted to clear Felicia's name so she can return to school and her normal life. I decided to do that even though I knew that Tristin had threatened to black-mail me." Devon grabbed her purse now, reaching for her cell phone. "I still have a few texts from Tristin on the night it all went down. She was very careful with her words, but if you take a look, you might get the gist." She opened the texts, showing them to Mrs. Dorman. "See? She was getting ready to threaten me with blackmail, but she only wanted to talk on the phone."

"Yes." Mrs. Dorman nodded. "That sounds believable enough. But people usually blackmail others by threatening to expose *corruption*, not innocence."

Cassidy stood now. "If that was true, why would Devon come in here like this? Why would she risk her neck when she could just sit back silently and get away with it? Why would she set herself up to get in serious trouble unless she truly was innocent?"

"That's right." Emma stood too. "We believe Devon is telling the truth. We believe she's risking everything just to help Felicia."

"And we think that's very admirable." Cassidy smiled at Devon.

"It's clear you girls are loyal to each other." Mrs. Dorman turned to Devon. "May I keep these things? Your phone and your laptop?"

"Sure." Devon nodded.

"Thanks to Felicia's dilemma, we now have access to an elec-tronic expert who can help us get to the bottom of this." Mrs. Dorman stood. "So unless you have a problem with someone digging around in your personal files, I'll ask them to see if they can validate your claims."

"If it will bring out the truth, I don't care who looks at it." Devon thought of something else. "Hey, do you think this expert could help me get that MyPlace page shut down? I hate the idea of it just sitting out there. I tried to shut it down myself—as soon as Tristin told me she'd put it up. But I couldn't get it down. I tried so many times that MyPlace finally banned me from their site. Your expert can find that on my computer too."

Mrs. Dorman made note of this. "I'll see what can be done. Thank you, girls, for coming in like this. Ask Miss Sharpe to give you a tardy excuse before you go."

"So I can go to class?" Devon asked her. "You're not kicking me out?"

Mrs. Dorman gave her a weary smile. "Not yet. If we find out that you've lied about this . . . well, we'll cross that bridge when we get there."

"You won't get there," Devon promised. "I haven't lied."

"What about Felicia?" Emma asked as they were going out. "Does she get to come back to school?"

"You'll be pleased to know that Felicia is supposed to be in class today." Mrs. Dorman smiled at them. "Get moving, girls, you're already fifteen minutes late."

As Devon hurried to class, she felt a smidgeon of hope. Okay, she wasn't exactly proud of all the things this electronic expert might find on her computer and phone, but she knew there was nothing she'd put there that could get her kicked out of school or in trouble with the law. Nothing besides the page that Tristin had put up anyway. Hopefully, they would figure this out.

have some happy news," Abby announced at lunch. "Kent officially asked me to the Christmas ball." She beamed at her friends, pleased that she was the first girl in the DG to secure a date. After congratulations were shared, Abby turned to Bryn. "So how about you? You're my double. Has a guy stepped up yet?"

"Jason keeps hinting." Bryn shrugged. "I suppose I could do worse."

"Jason?" Abby frowned in dismay. "Seriously?"

"I know we all thought the worst of him . . . before . . ." Bryn's gaze flickered to Devon and back to Abby. "But I've gotten to know him some, working on the dance committee, and really he's not so bad."

"You honestly think you'd go out with Jason?" Cassidy looked worried.

"Don't repeat this to anyone, but Amanda thinks Jason is going to ask her," Devon divulged.

"Hmm . . ." Bryn tilted her head to one side as if the stakes had suddenly gotten higher—or more interesting. "Amanda might be in for a surprise."

"Speaking of Amanda, is she still in the DG?" Abby quietly asked everyone. She didn't want to sound gossipy, but she'd overheard Amanda and Tristin in the restroom this morning.

"She hasn't said a word about it," Bryn told her. "She's been acting a little chilly."

"I think I know why," Abby confided. "It has to do with something I heard Tristin and Amanda talking about."

"What was it?" Emma asked.

"I don't like repeating it. What they said wasn't very nice." Abby made an apologetic grimace to Devon. "And your name was, uh, mentioned."

"How did you happen to overhear them?" Bryn asked curiously.

"I was in a restroom stall and they were talking. Naturally I didn't come out until they left."

"What did they say about me?" Devon demanded.

"I can't remember word for word, but the general insinuation was that you and Felicia were the same . . . that you were both, uh, skanks." Abby gave Devon an apologetic half smile. "They both seemed really annoyed that Felicia had been allowed back in school, and Tristin seemed fairly certain that you, Devon, are on your way out. To be honest, I suspect that Amanda's sort of in the dark as far as Tristin's role in the MyPlace scandal. At the same time, the things Amanda said . . . the way she said them . . . well, it was more than just mean."

"We don't need someone like that in the DG," Cassidy declared.

"What do we do?" Bryn asked. "It's not like we can just vote to kick Amanda out and not expect any backlash. We'll have to handle this really carefully."

"Speaking of those two, what's the latest on the Tristin situation?" Abby asked Devon. "Cassidy filled me in on the meeting with Mrs. Dorman. When will they get that all figured out?"

"I haven't heard a thing yet," Devon said a bit glumly.

"Back to Amanda and the DG," Emma said. "I want to make a motion that we vote Amanda out and vote Felicia in."

"Not so fast," Bryn told her. "This is something we should really think about. Especially in light of the Christmas ball. Amanda is helping with that. I don't want to alienate her. Especially not right before the assembly. No telling how she might sabotage that if she was in a snit. I suggest we don't deal with this until the MyPlace bit with Tristin shakes down. I move that we all just keep our mouths shut for a while."

"Bryn's right," Abby agreed. "We need to focus on the Christmas ball right now. Specifically Project Santa Sleigh. Kent and I were talking about this today. We've got lots of ideas. It's such a great opportunity to do some real good with down-and-out kids. We need to get everyone in the school fired up about helping, and Friday's assembly could do that. I've got a great program worked out. One that will knock everyone's socks off if we do it right. But I need everyone's full cooperation. Even Amanda's."

"Are you going to fill us in at this afternoon's meeting?" Bryn asked.

"Yes. We need to organize and do some rehearsing, and we have to swear everyone to secrecy. Especially in regard to our prizes."

"Good." Bryn nodded. "Don't let anyone steal our thunder. Save it until Friday."

"Speaking of the assembly . . ." Emma made an impish smile. "I found the other elf. Unless anyone objects, it's Felicia. She gladly agreed to help."

"Felicia would be perfect," Abby assured her.

"We're going to work on our costumes tonight," Emma told

them. She described the sleigh she was working on. "It's not a typical Santa sleigh at all. It's really bright and fun and crazy. A real rockin' out kinda sleigh."

"Sounds great." Abby said. "Maybe we could have you come out with some music. Something jazzy and fun . . . like 'Jingle Bell Rock.'"

"Awesome!" Bryn proclaimed.

Abby told them some of her other ideas for the assembly. She also told them about how she and Kent wanted to get a jump start on their project. "We plan to select our kids this weekend. Kent's already been helping at the FAC. That's the Family Assistance Center downtown. It's associated with the homeless shelter. Anyway, Kent volunteers on Saturdays. He just hangs in the gym, organizing sports and games with the kids. He says it's really fun." Abby beamed at them. "I'm going to help him on Saturday. We're hoping to pick out a kid or two—or three or four—that we can help."

"Very cool," Cassidy said.

"And we're putting together a list of resources," Abby continued, "different local organizations that assist children. We'll have them available for everyone who decides to participate in the contest."

"Which will be the only way they can get into the dance." Bryn grinned.

"This is so awesome," Emma said. "That motivates me even more to get my date with Isaac set in stone."

"Me too," Cassidy said.

"Is Lane getting warmer?" Emma asked her.

Cassidy shrugged. "He's friendly . . . like usual. But he hasn't mentioned the Christmas ball."

"Well, just wait until Friday," Bryn told them. "When everyone hears about our fabulous prizes—it'll change everything. People will be scrambling for dates and for double dates."

• • ● ● •

As chair of the Project Santa Sleigh committee, Abby knew there was a lot riding on her shoulders. In some ways it was more pressure than playing varsity basketball. At the same time, she knew she was naturally good at organizing. For the next couple of days, she carefully went over everything, crossing every *t* and dotting every *i*. Besides doing her regular schoolwork and making plans, with Kent's help, for Project Santa Sleigh, Friday's assembly was all she thought about.

By Friday morning, she felt fairly confident they were ready. But by that afternoon, as they waited backstage, she had to take several long, deep breaths to calm her frazzled nerves—and she prayed a silent prayer that nothing major would go wrong. There were so many ways this thing could flop and they could end up looking like total fools. If that happened, it wouldn't just ruin the success of the dance, but it might put the kibosh on what could possibly turn out to be one of the best Christmases for a lot of needy children. That was what was motivating her.

First Abby checked on Felicia and Emma. They looked adorable in their elf outfits, which had been repurposed from *Midsummer Night's Dream* costumes. Abby had helped them with some final details via Skype last night, and these two were the stylingest elves ever. Not only that, but the sleigh that Emma had created this week was totally awesome. As it turned out, since Cass was busy, Felicia had jumped in to help with it. The sled was painted with a shiny hot-pink base coat and embellished with a colorful design of swirling glitter and glitzy rhinestones. Plus it had battery-operated neon-colored Christmas lights that flashed off and on. It was like Barbie meets Santa on steroids.

"You guys ready?" Abby asked them.

Emma nodded eagerly, making the oversized bell on her purple pointed cap jingle merrily.

"This is so fun," Felicia exclaimed. "I'm so glad I got to help."

Abby went over to check on Jason. Even if she wasn't that fond of this guy, she appreciated his willingness to help out, and she had to admit he looked pretty swanky in his 1960s retro black tuxedo. Jason's role was to help kick this thing off with his "persona"—Amanda's idea since she claimed the whole school respected Jason. Abby thought that was debatable, but she'd had the good sense to keep her mouth shut on the matter. "Ready to rock and roll?" she asked him.

"Just as soon as my Christmas babes are ready." He pointed over to where Bryn and Amanda were just finishing up their primping. Both girls were dressed to the nines in glittery gowns that Formal Rental Wear had freely loaned them just for the day—with the promise that the dance committee would post some advertisements for the shop in gratitude.

Abby glanced out to the auditorium, seeing that it was nearly full now and spotting Mr. Worthington making his way up to the stage. The crowd quieted some as he adjusted the mike and started to make the usual announcements in his slightly monotone voice, which some swore was more effective than a sleeping pill. Finally he finished up and, using the same monotone, introduced Abby.

Abby was dressed just like any normal day at school. She slowly sauntered up to the mike, acting like there was no big deal, like she wasn't really into this—which was all just part of the act.

"Hey, everyone," she began in a ho-hum sort of tone that was strangely similar to Worthington's. "As you know it's that time of year again. Time to start thinking about this year's Christmas ball." She feigned a bored yawn. "I know, I know, this has been the least attended event in Northwood history and it will probably be even—"

Suddenly some lively, upbeat music started to play, drowning

Melody Carlson

out Abby's boring monologue. She turned in alarm, pretending to be surprised and confused as Jason danced onto the stage with Bryn on one arm and Amanda on the other. All three of them were doing a fabulous job of rocking out—they'd obviously worked on some dance moves. The crowd responded with clapping and cheering, obviously relieved to be rescued from Abby's boring announcement.

The dance continued for about thirty seconds, and between Jason's suave tux, Bryn's shimmering scarlet dress, and Amanda's emerald-green sequins, the threesome looked really festive. Abby just frowned, holding up her hands like it was useless as she exited the stage.

As the music died down, the threesome took over the mike and started up some scripted bantering over which girl Jason would escort to the dance. This skit had been Abby's idea and was actually pretty apropos, not to mention amusing—since Jason wanted to take Bryn, but Amanda actually wanted to go with Jason. The plan was to use this situation to announce that the Christmas ball was going to be for double dates.

"Come on," Jason pleaded with the audience. "There's gotta be a guy out there who'd like to get in on this. Look—I've got two gorgeous girls and as much as I'd like to take them both, I need a guy to step up and—"

"I'll take Bryn," a male voice yelled from the audience.

Bryn waved and smiled. "Thank you!"

"That's wonderful," Amanda said into the mike now. "So it looks like there will be at least one double date for the dance." She did a quick head count. "That makes four."

Bryn stepped up now. "But four doesn't make much of a party. Hopefully some others out there will want to join us. To sweeten the deal a bit, we've got an exciting announcement." She poked Jason in the chest. "We girls know what cheapskates most of you guys are."

161

Jason gave her a shocked, innocent look then pulled out his pockets to show they were empty. "Hey, I can't help it if I'm broke."

"Well, the good news for you guys is that the dance is *free!*" Bryn exclaimed.

This elicited some cheers, mostly from the girls by the sounds of it.

"So no one has the ticket price for an excuse," Amanda told them as the music started up again—and now the threesome danced their way off the stage. This was Abby's cue to come back.

She knew this was the serious part of the assembly and she'd just been praying it would go off without a hitch. At least the audience seemed a little more attentive now. She could tell they were curious. Kent and Isaac had used their TV and video class to help her produce a short video—kind of like a PSA. "Now that we have your attention," she told the audience, "we want to share this with you." She nodded to the screen behind her and just like that, the video began to play, showing photos of children in less than desirable living situations. They had sad faces, and combined with the narrative that Abby had recorded earlier, their lives sounded rather bleak and hopeless. The auditorium was silent when the video ended.

"I know this video seems like a shocking contrast when we're talking about something like a slightly decadent Christmas ball," she began somberly. "I doubt that anyone in this room can truly relate to the kind of poverty these children experience every single day of their lives—or the disappointment they will feel when Santa seems to have forgotten them . . . again. So I want to take a moment to ask every single one of you to consider this question: What can you do to help a needy child during the upcoming Christmas season?"

As planned, the stage went dark for a few seconds. The auditorium was silent—as if the crowd was actually considering her challenge. Then suddenly the lights came on and, with "Jingle Bell Rock" playing, the two stylish elves danced out towing their flashy sleigh. Emma and Felicia were boogying and jumping around—until they stopped center stage and bent over to peer into the sleigh. Exclaiming that it was empty, the two girls collapsed into loud sobs and the cheery music dwindled, replaced by an old Elvis tune about having a blue, blue Christmas.

Abby could tell that the audience was both amused and confused. Perfect.

Feeling confident that her mission was nearly accomplished, Abby returned to the mike. This time she spoke with excited animation. "Okay, everyone, you heard that the Christmas ball is free this year. But now I'm going to tell you exactly how and why it's free." Abby explained Project Santa Sleigh and how every double date was expected to create some kind of sleigh and to fill it with gifts for needy children. "That will be considered your admission into the dance. But that's not all." She held up a finger. "You and your dates will be expected to adopt a child or two or even a family, and everything you put into your sleigh will be delivered to them—helping them to have a truly wonderful Christmas."

As Abby finished, Amanda and Bryn and Jason danced back onto the stage and when the music faded, Bryn grabbed the mike. "Well, that's all fine and good, but it sounds like a lot of work to me—making a sleigh, filling it with stuff, finding kids who need some help." She turned to Amanda. "Doncha think?"

Amanda nodded as she took the mike, pointing at the audience. "The truth is, we were a little worried that some of you lazy people might think this way too. So we decided you might need a little motivation, ya know?" She handed the mike to Jason.

"That's why we decided to turn Project Santa Sleigh into a *contest*!" He announced this like a contest in itself was fabulous motivation. "I can't speak for you girls, but we guys tend to love competition. So everyone will be challenged to create the coolest sleigh, filled with the coolest stuff. Impartial judges will pick one double-date foursome as the winners." He looked expectantly out to the crowd.

"Well, if it's a contest, shouldn't there be a prize?" Amanda asked.

"Yeah." Bryn nodded. "We need a prize."

"Is that right?" Jason called out to the crowd. "You guys think we need a prize?"

Everyone clapped and cheered.

"Well, it just so happens we've got some pretty cool prizes." Jason continued building it up. "Since we knew you guys might be among the least motivated, we decided we needed something really off the hook to get you into this." He made a dramatic pause. "You ready for this? Tell me, guys, have any of you ever been to the *Rose Bowl* before?" Naturally the crowd went wild. "That's right. We just happen to have two expenses-paid trips to the Rose Bowl—that's the prize for the male side of the winning double date."

"Hey," Amanda said, "what about the girls?"

"That's right," Bryn added. "What about the girls?"

"You think girls wanna go to the Rose Bowl?" Jason frowned.

"No," Bryn told him. "The girls I know would much rather go to something like . . . well, something like the *red carpet at the Oscars*. Right, girls?" The girls in the audience cheered loudly.

"Well, how about that. I just happen to have—" Jason held up two fingers—"two tickets for an expenses-paid trip to the Oscars red carpet event—in *Hollywood*!"

Just as planned, confetti and streamers fell onto the stage as the music started to play loudly. The elves and the threesome danced happily about and everyone in the auditorium erupted in loud applause and enthusiastic cheers.

When it all died down, Bryn grabbed the mike again. "Okay, everyone, you know what this means. Get your double dates lined up and start working on Project Santa Sleigh. We'll have lots more information about the rules of the contest as well as resources for finding your children to help on the school's website."

"Let the games begin!" Jason made a fist pump and the crowd continued to clap.

Abby couldn't have been more pleased when she finally exited the auditorium. Everything had gone off perfectly. The response from the crowd was even better than expected. As she headed for her locker, noticing the Christmas ball and Project Santa Sleigh posters that had been hung by some of the committee members while the assembly took place, she felt certain this project was off to a great start.

"Nice job."

Abby turned in surprise to see her dad coming from behind her. "What are you doing here?" she asked.

"Your mother told me about how hard you've been working to put this assembly together. I had some time so I thought I'd pop in to see what you were up to." He put an arm around her shoulders, giving her a warm squeeze. "I'm proud of you, honey."

"Even though I gave up basketball?"

He made a crooked grin then nodded. "I think you made the right choice. I can't wait to see how Project Santa Sleigh turns out."

Abby couldn't remember a happier moment as her dad walked her toward her locker. Now if only this whole thing would go off as smoothly as the assembly.

That was so awesome!" Felicia exclaimed as she and Emma went backstage to change out of their elf outfits. "Thanks for letting me do it with you."

"Thank *you*," Emma said with enthusiasm. "It was a whole lot easier to go out there and act like goofballs with you by my side."

"*Goofballs?*" Felicia acted offended, then laughed. "Yeah, it was pretty silly, but it was still fun."

"Thanks for helping with the sleigh too," Emma said as she pulled off her cap.

"All I did was follow directions and glue things where you said to."

"Well, it wouldn't have been nearly as glitzy without your help." As Emma peeled off the magenta velveteen vest, she thought about Cassidy. She had been trying not to complain, but so far Cass had not been pulling her weight in regard to Project Santa Sleigh. Emma knew it was because Cass had been so focused on midterms and, being the academic of the group,

Cassidy always took a heavier load of classes. But even so, it felt unbalanced and slightly unfair.

"I just hope that I'll get a chance to be part of a double date," Felicia said a bit glumly.

"Why wouldn't you?"

"Because of that stupid MyPlace page." Felicia let out a long sigh. "What guy would want to ask me out now?"

"Well, that's just wrong." Emma pulled on her jeans. "I'm surprised Tristin hasn't gotten in trouble for it yet."

"Maybe she didn't really do it." Felicia zipped her hoodie. "Remember a person should be considered innocent until proven guilty."

"Yeah . . . right." Emma grimaced to remember how Felicia hadn't been treated like that. "So do you still want to join our, uh, our club?"

Felicia's eyes lit up. "Really? You guys will let me?"

"I think so." Emma pulled on a boot. "I'll have to check with the others, but the last time we talked about it, everyone had been open to it. Now that your name's been cleared . . ."

"Does that mean you guys will help me find a date to the dance?" Felicia asked hopefully.

Emma shrugged as she reached for her phone. "I can't promise anything." She sent a quick text to the other DG members, asking them if they could have a brief meeting today or tomorrow. By the time she and Felicia were wheeling the sleigh toward the parking lot where Cassidy had promised to meet them to give them a ride home, the DG had already agreed to meet at Costello's at four. Naturally, Emma couldn't invite Felicia to this meeting.

"The assembly was awesome," Cassidy said cheerfully as she drove to Felicia's house. "You guys were great little elves."

"It was really fun," Felicia said. "I was kinda sad when it was all over."

"Maybe it's not all over," Cassidy told them. "I heard Abby saying that she's going to ask you to be elves again for the skating party."

"Skating party?" Felicia asked.

Cass told Felicia about the plan to invite all the kids involved in Project Santa Sleigh to a skating party to present the gifts.

"Naturally, that won't happen until after the Christmas ball," Emma clarified as Cassidy pulled up to Felicia's house.

"I really hope I get to go—I mean, go to the dance and be part of a double date and do the competition and help the kids and everything." Felicia crossed her fingers as she got out of the car. "Even if I don't get asked to the dance, it was fun helping you guys today." She smiled brightly.

"Thanks again," Emma called out.

"She's so sweet," Cassidy said as she drove away.

"I know. It just doesn't seem fair that she should miss out on the dance—especially after she's been so much help with everything."

"Yeah, I know." Cassidy grinned at Emma. "Speaking of the dance, I have good news."

"What?"

"Lane asked me to go with him! After seeing that video that Isaac and Kent put together, he's super excited about Project Santa Sleigh. And even more so after he heard about the prizes. It's like our plan is really working."

"Uh-huh." As much as she hated being like this, Emma was starting to feel slightly resentful toward Cassidy again. Here she'd gotten a date to the dance, but she'd done hardly a thing to help with Project Santa Sleigh.

"That doesn't sound very enthusiastic." Cassidy frowned at Emma. "I thought you'd be happier for me."

"I am." Emma tried to inject mirth into her tone. "Lucky you."

"Lucky you too." Cassidy giggled. "Don't say you heard this from me, but Lane hinted that Isaac will be asking you soon."

Emma couldn't help but smile. "Well, that is good news. I still feel sad for Felicia, though." She told Cassidy about Felicia's concerns that no guy would want to take her. "In fact, that's why I called this meeting. I want Felicia to be part of the DG."

"Hopefully everyone will agree with you," Cassidy said as she parked in front of Costello's. "Just in case, you should be ready to make your case." She pointed at a small red car. "Looks like Amanda is here too."

"I still don't feel like she belongs in the DG," Emma said quietly as they walked toward the coffeehouse.

"Yeah, I know." Cass pulled open the door.

Soon they were seated with the other girls. Before Emma could present Felicia's case and ask for a vote, Amanda took over. "Did you guys hear the news yet?" she asked eagerly.

"What news?" Devon asked.

"Tristin's been expelled."

"Seriously?" Bryn's blue eyes grew wide. "So she really did make the MyPlace page on Felicia?"

"So it seems." Amanda scowled. "I had my suspicions all along, but Tristin kept telling me it wasn't her."

"How do you know it was her?" Abby asked.

"She confessed." Amanda grimly shook her head. "Stupid, stupid girl."

"Stupid for confessing?" Emma demanded.

"No. Stupid for doing it."

"Why *did* she do it?" Abby asked.

Amanda shrugged. "Who knows?"

"Because she's mean," Emma declared. "Just plain mean."

"And because of Marcus Zimmerman," Cassidy added. "Because Tristin was into Marcus and he had been looking at Felicia. Tristin smeared Felicia."

"Speaking of Felicia," Emma said quickly, before they all went down another rabbit trail, "that's why I called this meeting. I want to nominate her for membership."

"You gotta be kidding," Amanda said.

"No. I'm not." Emma frowned at Amanda. "In fact, I suspect if Tristin hadn't done what she did, Felicia would already be a member."

"But that will make the DG an odd number," Bryn pointed out. "What about the double date plan?"

"Speaking of the double date plan," Devon said carefully, "I still need someone to double with me."

"I thought you and Amanda were—"

"That was *before* . . ." Amanda's brows arched slightly.

"Before *what*?" Devon demanded.

"Before you did exactly what Tristin did." Amanda glared at Devon.

"I admit it was stupid. I only did it to help clear Felicia's name."

"Two wrongs don't make a right," Amanda said haughtily.

"Okay, okay." Cassidy held up one hand as she clicked on her iPad. "Let's not turn this into a fight. Maybe it's time to go over the DG rules again."

They all let out a moan.

"Fine," Cassidy said. "But we were discussing voting in a new member. Let's deal with that before we move on to other business."

Emma took the opportunity to make a quick impassioned plea for Felicia, reminding the girls of how she'd been slandered and expelled and then how she'd enthusiastically helped with the assembly today. "And she helped with making the sleigh too." She glanced at Cassidy. "You should be grateful for that."

Cass frowned. "Yeah . . . well, let's put it to a vote. All in favor?" Everyone except Amanda put up a hand.

"Amanda?" Emma said with irritation.

"Well, I'm just thinking," Amanda said slowly. "If Felicia joins the DG, who will partner with her on the double date?"

No one said anything for a moment.

"I will," Emma declared.

"But you're with me," Cassidy reminded her.

"Felicia already helped me make the sleigh," Emma gently pointed out. "And she helped me in the assembly today. Maybe it makes more sense for me to partner with her."

"Yeah . . . I guess that makes sense." But Cassidy looked both shocked and hurt.

Emma glanced back at Amanda now. "Especially since no one else wants to partner with Felicia. Now will you vote for her?"

"I'm still not sure," Amanda said stubbornly.

"We need a unanimous vote," Cassidy pointed out. "We still don't have it."

Devon nudged Cassidy. "I'll partner with you," she said eagerly. "I think Harris is going to ask me to the dance. He was actually flirting with me after the assembly."

"Harris Martin is asking you?" Amanda said in disbelief.

"Maybe." Devon looked uncertain.

"If we let Felicia in," Bryn said slowly, "it'll be Emma and Felicia, Cassidy and Devon, and Abby and me." She glanced at Amanda.

"What about me?" Amanda said in a slightly whiny tone.

"What about you?" Devon said nonchalantly. "You turned up your nose at me. Now it appears there's no one left."

"What about Sienna?" Bryn suggested. "She'll be without a partner now that Tristin's expelled."

"But she's not in the DG," Cassidy pointed out.

"Maybe that doesn't matter," Emma added. "It's not like—"

"Why *can't* Sienna be in the DG?" Amanda demanded. "If we vote Felicia in, why not vote Sienna in too? She's interested. In fact, I'll vote for Felicia if you guys let Sienna in."

"Isn't that like blackmail?" Emma asked the others.

"I think Amanda needs to make a case for Sienna—just like Emma did for Felicia," Devon told them.

Amanda sat up straighter. "Fine. I will. For starters Sienna is a very nice person. She's very honest and hardworking and smart."

"I can vouch for the last part," Cassidy told them. "I have Sienna in some classes. She is hardworking and smart."

"Here's something you may not know," Amanda said quietly. "Sienna has never been on a real date."

"Seriously?" Devon looked shocked. "But she's so pretty and popular."

"Her parents wouldn't let her date until she turned seventeen."

"Well, she's a senior," Cassidy pointed out. "How old is she?"

"Seventeen." Amanda took a sip of coffee.

"Does she have a date for the dance?" Bryn asked.

"Not yet, but she wants to go." Amanda pointed at them. "And that's how the DG can help."

"Helping Sienna get a date should be easy enough," Bryn told her.

"Says you," Abby teased. "Don't forget you haven't gotten yourself a date yet."

"I could go with Jason if I wanted to," Bryn pointed out.

"Then why don't you?" Amanda challenged her.

"Because I don't want to." Bryn stuck out her chin.

"Back to Sienna and Felicia," Cassidy said grumpily. "Some of us don't have all night, you know."

They discussed it all some more, but before the meeting adjourned, they had admitted two new members—and everyone seemed to be fairly happy about it. Everyone except Cassidy, that is. As Cass drove Emma home, she seemed to be in a serious snit.

"Are you mad that I'm partnering with Felicia on this?" Emma asked when Cassidy pulled up to her house.

"Not exactly mad . . . just hurt." Cassidy turned to look at Emma. "I feel kind of blindsided."

"But no one else wanted to go with Felicia."

"I know."

"And she'd been helping me already."

"Yeah." Cassidy let out a sigh. "I'll be okay with it, Em."

"You and Devon have been getting along pretty good lately," Emma said encouragingly.

Cassidy frowned. "Yeah . . . lately. But you never know what Devon might pull."

"I'm sure you'll keep her in line," Emma said as she opened the door.

"Right. Babysitting Devon—just what I want to do."

"It'll all work out, Cass." Emma grinned. "Don't forget, at least you have a *real* date. You should be celebrating that Lane asked you out. Remember?"

Cassidy brightened. "That's true. It might be interesting getting to know Devon better too. She might be unpredictable, but she sometimes comes up with some pretty clever ideas. You're right. It'll be okay."

As Emma went into the house, she felt a little uncertain—or maybe even a little jealous. Had she been too hasty to let go of her partnership with Cassidy? After all, Cassidy was smart and motivated and trustworthy. For all Emma knew, Felicia might not even want to partner with Emma.

She peeled off her coat and pulled out her phone. She wanted to call Felicia and share the good news, but before she did this, she noticed she had a text from Isaac. He was asking if she had a date to the Christmas ball yet. Feeling excited at the prospect, she texted him back her answer then waited.

In less than a minute Isaac texted back, inviting her to go with him. Okay, she might've preferred being asked in person or even on the phone. But maybe this was for the best . . . considering it was Isaac. So now she texted him back saying she would only go with him on two conditions: one, she wanted to double with Felicia, and two, Isaac had to get Marcus Zimmerman to ask her out. This time she waited for five minutes with no response.

Feeling saddened that she might've frightened him off, Emma decided to go ahead and call Felicia anyway. First she told her the good news, explaining more fully about what the Dating Games club was and even reading her the rules. "So do you want to be part of it?"

"Are you kidding?" Felicia sounded elated. "Of course I do."

"Okay, that's the good news," Emma told her.

"There's bad news?"

"Well, we still don't have dates for the Christmas ball." Emma thought about Isaac's delayed response in regard to her "conditions."

"At least we have a sleigh," Felicia said optimistically. "I already have some ideas for things we can put inside it."

"Really?" Emma said with interest. "Like what?"

Felicia told her about some possibilities, and they both started coming up with more ideas. By the time Emma hung up, she didn't even feel all that concerned that Isaac hadn't gotten back to her yet. Surely there would be a couple of nice guys at Northwood who'd be interested in taking her and Felicia to the dance.

Bryn felt somewhat dismayed as she got ready for school on Monday, or maybe she was simply confused. It seemed like the rest of the DG was getting their dates all set for the Christmas ball. Everyone but Bryn! How could that be? As everyone knew, Abby had already secured a date with Kent, and then Cassidy got asked by Lane on Friday. On Saturday, Devon texted the DG, smugly announcing that she'd managed to snag Harris Martin for her date. Harris had been one of Bryn's options—or so she'd imagined. That certainly hadn't been easy to swallow.

Then to make Bryn feel even worse, she'd learned just yesterday that Emma had been asked by Isaac. According to Emma, Isaac had encouraged Marcus Zimmerman to ask Felicia. So they were all squared away too. Five girls with dates! As Bryn put the finishing touches on her already perfect hair and makeup, she studied her reflection. *What's wrong with me?*

As she drove to Abby's house to pick her up for school, she was well aware that Jason was perfectly willing to take her to the dance. But she was still uneasy about that. The memory of how he'd treated Devon continued to haunt her. Or maybe it was her pride. She would never admit it to anyone, but why would she want to go out with Devon's castoff? Or was that really how it went down? More confusion. Despite the fact that Jason was acting like a perfect gentleman toward her, Bryn just couldn't be sure. Besides that, it seemed that everyone in the DG was opposed to her going with him.

"Are you upset about something?" Abby asked after they'd ridden in silence together.

"Oh . . ." Bryn forced a smile. "Not really. It's just a little disturbing that everyone has a date for the dance but me—the chairman of the Christmas ball." She shuddered. "How is that going to look?"

"You *have* to get a date," Abby insisted. "To attend the dance and enter the contest, we need you to be the other half of our double date."

"Believe me, I know."

"Kent and I already started to work on Project Santa Sleigh."

"Did you start making the sleigh yet?"

"No, but there's plenty of time for that later." Abby told Bryn about some of the things they'd done during the weekend, how they'd spent time at the Family Assistance Center, playing and getting to know some of the kids. "We even picked out a brother and sister that we'd like to help. Sarita and Samuel. I have photos of them on my phone. Sarita is seven and very smart. Samuel is five and just adorable. We've already made a list of specific ways we plan to help them. It's so fun, Bryn. You need to be part of this."

"I know, I know." Bryn let out a loud sigh as she turned into the school parking lot. As they got out, Abby continued prattling on about this brother and sister, who really did sound sweet. But all Bryn could think about was that she needed to snag herself a date—before there was nothing left to choose.

"I was thinking," Bryn said quietly as they went through the front entrance. "If I get really desperate, I could probably entice Darrell Zuckerman to ask me to the dance."

Abby chuckled like this was funny. "Yeah, I bet you could."

"Okay, I realize he's kind of nerdy."

"I never said that," Abby said defensively. "I happen to like Darrell a lot. I'm just surprised that you were thinking of him."

"Well, he's very intelligent, and to be honest, he was a pretty good date at the masquerade ball."

"Who are you talking about?" Devon asked as she joined them.

"Bryn is thinking about Darrell for her date for the—"

"I am *not*." Bryn sent Abby a warning look.

"Why not?" Devon elbowed Bryn with a teasing expression. "You could do worse."

"Thanks for your support." Bryn glared at Devon.

Devon laughed. "Okay, I'll admit that I don't remember a lot about that masquerade dance, but it seemed like Darrell made a nice-looking Gatsby."

"He would make a perfectly fine date," Abby insisted. "And I bet he'd be really good help for Project Santa Sleigh too. I'm sure he and Kent would get along. Want me to go drop some hints?"

"No," Bryn snapped at her. "Thanks but no thanks."

Abby blinked, then nodded. "Sure . . . whatever."

• ● ● ● •

Bryn felt even more downhearted by the time she went into the cafeteria for lunch. It seemed that Friday's assembly had been a complete and unprecedented success. As a result it seemed like everyone in the entire school had dates for the dance already. Okay, she knew she was over-blowing this whole thing in her head. But was it possible that the chair for the Christmas ball would be left on the sidelines?

"Why so glum, chum?" Devon asked her as Bryn set her sack lunch on the table and sat down.

Bryn turned to Devon with a pasted on smile. "I'm not glum."

"Oh, good." Devon opened a bag of chips. "I have some news that might cheer you up . . . or make you laugh."

"What's that?" Bryn asked hopefully.

"Well, I was telling Amanda about how we were teasing you about Darrell Zuckerman and—"

"You told Amanda that?"

"Hey, hear me out."

"What?" Bryn waited, wondering if they had gone ahead and set her up with Darrell . . . and thinking that perhaps that wouldn't even be such a bad thing after all. Really, Darrell had been a fun date.

"Amanda got the brilliant idea to get Darrell for Sienna and—"

"*What?*"

Devon pointed to where Amanda and Sienna were hurrying over to their table. "Maybe we'll hear how it went."

"Sienna has a date," Amanda announced.

"Darrell?" Devon asked.

"That's right," Sienna confirmed. She grinned at Bryn. "I figured if he was good enough for you—I mean, for the last dance—he would be good enough for me."

"Well, that sounds romantic," Devon teased.

"I actually like Darrell," Sienna told them. "But I never really thought of him as dating material." She laughed. "Not that I've had any experience."

"What about you?" Devon asked Amanda. "Do you have a date yet?"

Amanda scowled at Bryn. "That depends on her."

"On me?" Bryn asked her.

Amanda nodded with a victorious gleam in her eye. "I've

gotten a confirmation from Jason that if you don't agree to go with him by the end of the day, he's taking me. Since you've already made it clear to everyone"—Amanda glanced at the others—"that you have no intention of going with Jason, I think it's a done deal."

"What do you mean I've *made it clear*?" Bryn demanded.

Amanda gave her a patronizing smile. "Remember what you told us on Friday, Bryn? At the meeting at Costello's? You said you were definitely not going with him." Amanda waved to the rest of the DG at the table. "Right, girls?"

Everyone sort of conceded that this was true, and to be honest, Bryn remembered making a statement to that effect. "Well, it's possible that I've changed my mind."

Amanda's eyes narrowed. "What about the DG rules?"

"What about them?"

"Rule number six. We will never steal a fellow DG's boyfriend," Amanda recited.

"Wow, someone's been doing her homework," Cassidy remarked.

"What about it?" Amanda pressed Bryn.

"For starters, Jason is not your boyfriend and—"

"He used to be. Maybe we were working toward it again." Amanda made a wounded look. "Until you stepped in."

"That's ridiculous." Bryn frowned.

Sienna tapped Amanda on the shoulder. "I have to agree with her, Amanda."

Amanda glared at Sienna.

"Come on, Amanda, you know it's not true. You and Jason weren't getting back together. You only got interested in him after you saw that he was interested in Bryn."

"That goes against rule number five," Cassidy pointed out, "about not being jealous over a DG's boyfriend."

Amanda made a little sigh. "Okay, whatever." She pointed

at Bryn now. "But Jason sounded serious. He's giving you until the end of the day to decide."

Bryn just shook her head, trying to appear nonchalant, but underneath her smooth surface, she felt very uneasy. No way was she going to let Amanda steal the last available date in the school from her. No way!

· · ● · ·

Jason caught up with Bryn as she was coming out of her last class. She completely expected him to beg her to go to the dance with him, but instead he told her that Jack and Beth wanted to meet with them right after school. "Beth left a message on my phone," he said nervously. "She didn't say why they want to meet, but something about it feels kinda urgent to me."

"Oh dear." Bryn shoved a paperback into her bag. "You don't think they're going to back out on the prizes for the dance, do you?"

"That would be rough if they did." Jason frowned. "Everyone is so on board with the whole contest thing. I'd hate to have to pull the plug."

"We'd just have to round up some new prizes," Bryn said with determination. "Jack and Beth aren't the only rich people in this town."

"No . . . they're just the richest." Jason chuckled. "Wanna ride with me?"

"You have your mom's car?"

"No. I drove my Jeep." He rolled his eyes. "It's still pretty muddy from this weekend. I went four-wheeling with Harris on Saturday."

"I'll drive."

"Okay."

"Meet me in the parking lot," she commanded. "Five minutes."

He made a mock salute. "Yes, ma'am."

Bryn made a quick stop in the restroom. Mostly to check her hair and makeup, because she wanted to look perfect. For the Hartfords, yes—that was important—but mostly for Jason. Somehow she had to get him to ask her to the dance again. Without her hinting, since she knew that could come back to haunt her. She had to make it seem like she was reluctantly agreeing to this. Like he had twisted her arm. How else could she save face around her friends?

They made small talk as Bryn drove, but it wasn't long until they were discussing various details about the dance. However, it felt more like a planning meeting than a prelude to an invitation. By the time Bryn was parking in front of the Hartfords' house, she was starting to wonder if Jason had already given up on her. Perhaps he'd already secured a date with Amanda. After all, he and Amanda had gone together for a long time last year. It wasn't hard to imagine they could've ignited that old flame. Naturally, this made Bryn feel even more uneasy . . . and jealous.

The dogs emerged, tumbling over each other and barking wildly again, just like last time. The housekeeper shushed the dogs, then welcomed Bryn and Jason into the house, leading them to a dimly lit library with walls filled with books and a fire burning in the fireplace. "I'll get Mr. and Mrs. Hartford."

"This is like something from an old movie," Bryn said as she gazed around the charming space.

"It's Jack's favorite place in the house," Jason said as he made himself comfortable in one of the deep leather chairs.

Bryn sat in the chair adjacent from Jason. She couldn't help but feel impressed with Jason's connection to these people, the way Jason seemed to fit so seamlessly into their world. And suddenly she wondered why on earth she'd been putting this guy off. For starters, he was good-looking. Very good-looking. Besides that he was wealthy. And—based on her own experience with him—he was relatively well mannered too. What was holding her back?

"You look perplexed," he said.

"Huh?" She looked up in surprise. "Oh . . . sorry . . . just thinking."

"About?"

She pressed her lips tightly together. "Oh . . . you know . . . the dance."

"Worried that we're about to get the rug pulled out from under us?" he teased.

"A little."

He frowned. "Yeah . . . I know. But I can't imagine that Jack and Beth would do—"

"Hello, hello," Jack said as he and his wife entered the room.

"Sorry to keep you waiting," Beth said a bit breathlessly. She was dressed in riding clothes and her cheeks were flushed.

"I'll bet you've been out with those beautiful horses," Bryn said.

Beth grinned. "You'd win that bet."

"Sorry to make you drive all the way out here for this." Jack sat down behind the big antique desk. "I'm getting ready to fly to LA and I wanted to see you kids face-to-face before I left."

"No problem," Jason said easily. "What's up?"

"First of all, we heard wonderful things about your assembly last week," Beth said graciously. "Kudos to both of you."

"Yes." Jack picked up a pen, balancing it in his fingers. "Mr. Worthington and I played golf on Saturday and he was quite impressed with what you kids have put together. Although he did ask me to verify the prizes for him." He chuckled. "Poor guy—he couldn't quite believe it. But I assured him the prizes are in earnest."

"Oh . . . good." Jason nodded.

"Mr. Worthington had some concerns with how the contest

would be judged. He wants to make sure that it's fair. As I'm sure you do too."

"Absolutely," Bryn assured him.

"So Beth and I have offered to handle the judging. Is that acceptable to you?"

"Of course," Jason agreed.

"That sounds perfect," Bryn told him.

"We might select a panel to help us," Beth told them. "If you don't mind."

"That would be wonderful," Bryn confessed. "In fact, it takes the pressure off of us."

"Oh, good." Beth made a relieved smile. "I was worried that you might feel we were being overly involved. Normally we like to be more hands-off. But we do care about Northwood, and we want this event to be a success. So as long as the committee chairs are not opposed, we'll proceed in this direction."

"Which means we'll be attending your dance." Jack laid down the pen, pushing his chair back.

"Only the first part of the dance," Beth assured them. "Don't worry, we won't make pests of ourselves."

"You'd be welcome for the whole thing," Bryn told her. "I hope you'll stay as long as you like."

"Well, it will be fun to see all the sleighs—to see what the kids have managed to put together. Such a good cause." Beth shrugged. "That's all we wanted to speak to you about." She looked at Jack. "I know you need to be heading to the airport soon."

He stood. "Thanks for coming out here on such short notice."

They all shook hands, and soon Bryn and Jason were out on the road again. "Well, that's a relief," Bryn said as she turned onto the main highway. "Whew."

Jason laughed. "Yeah, I didn't really think they were pulling the plug. But you never know."

"They're such nice people."

"Yeah, for rich folks, they're not so bad."

"You say that like your parents aren't wealthy too, Jason."

"Trust me, there's a big difference."

"Right." This simply reminded her there was a big difference between her own family's circumstances and Jason's. In fact, Amanda's family would be more in Jason's category of wealth than Bryn's. Thinking this just made Bryn feel more determined to secure a date with this guy. Still, she didn't want to be the one to bring it up. She couldn't let him know how desperate she was feeling.

As they got closer to the school, she got more nervous. They had talked about everything in regard to the dance and the promotions and the contest and the prizes and everything— everything except for who they were going with. Now they were at the school and he was getting out of her car, and she knew it was too late.

"Jason," she called as she got out of her car.

"Yeah?"

She stood by the driver's door, looking at him over the roof of her car. "I, um, I'm just curious about something."

"What?" He leaned his elbows on the roof of her car, studying her.

"Is it true you're taking Amanda to the dance?"

He looked puzzled.

"She mentioned your ultimatum."

"Ultimatum?"

"You know . . ."

He cocked his head to one side. "Huh?"

"She said you were taking her to the dance if I turned you down."

He shrugged. "I guess I said something like that."

"Oh . . ." She just nodded. "Okay."

"So did you turn me down?" he asked.

She smiled brightly. "Did you *really* ask me? I mean in a sincere and proper sort of way?"

His brow creased. "Huh?"

"Oh, well . . . never mind." She ducked her head down, getting back into her car. As she slid into the driver's seat, Jason got back in on the passenger's side.

"Okay, Miss Bryn Jacobs, will you honor me by going to the Christmas ball with me?" He gave a genuine-looking smile. "Please?"

She returned his smile. "Certainly."

Then, to her surprise, he leaned over the console and kissed her—right on the lips. "Cool." Without saying another word, he hopped out of her car and, waving happily, trotted over to a muddy red Jeep parked several rows away. As she restarted her car, she felt uncertain about everything—especially about the kiss. What did this mean? What had she gotten herself into? Then she remembered how comfortable he seemed with the Hartfords . . . impressive. And this, combined with her desperation not to remain dateless, made her decide it was all good. Before she drove away, she quickly texted the good news to her friends. Including Amanda.

For the past couple of days, Abby had kept her mouth shut over Bryn's decision to go to the dance with Jason, but beneath her tolerant veneer, she believed Bryn was making a big mistake. Still, she knew Bryn wouldn't listen to her concerns. Especially after Bryn had lashed into Devon when she'd expressed her opinion yesterday. That's when Abby decided to simply keep her mouth shut altogether. She consoled herself that they'd be on a double date, so it wasn't like Jason could pull some crazy stunt with Bryn. Not with Abby and Kent around. Plus, as Bryn kept claiming, maybe Jason did respect her more than he'd respected Devon.

Even so, Abby felt like Bryn was changing. Bryn had always been a lot more materialistic than Abby, but it seemed like she was becoming more shallow recently. She kept talking about the Hartfords and how rich they were. She even seemed to esteem Jason more highly just because his family was wealthy. Then there was the way she treated Amanda and Sienna—like they were more significant than her old friends. Abby had sort of understood when Bryn had catered to Amanda this week. Especially since Amanda was in such a snit over the news about Jason. Bryn had practically bent over backward to make amends with Amanda, doling out compliments and pleasantries until Abby thought she was going to gag. Fortunately Amanda had finally decided to ask a Northwood alumnus to accompany her.

"Can you guys meet at Costello's after school today?" Bryn asked the rest of the DG at lunch on Wednesday.

"What for?" Devon asked.

"To make plans for the dance. As you know, tomorrow's Thanksgiving, and I don't know about you girls, but I'm going to do some serious shopping on Black Friday."

"You mean you're shopping for Project Santa Sleigh?" Abby asked eagerly. She'd been hoping to get Bryn more on board for this. "I've started making a list and—"

"No. I mean I'm shopping for formals. I saw that Nordstrom's is having a big sale and—"

"I'm going to FRW for my dress," Emma announced.

"FRW?" Bryn frowned. "Huh?"

"Formal Rental Wear," Emma reminded her. "The ones who loaned you and Amanda the dresses for the assembly last week."

"You're going to *rent* a formal?" Bryn looked disgusted.

"Why not?" Cassidy chimed in. "Why put out so much money for a dress you'll wear only once?"

"Seriously?" Amanda frowned. "I mean, it was okay for the assembly, but for the Christmas ball?"

"It's a great idea." Felicia nodded at Emma. "I'm going to FRW too."

Now the girls became almost equally divided and the argument was on. Emma, Felicia, and Cassidy refused to back down from their frugal plans and were already agreeing to get a jump start by going rental gown shopping right after school that day.

Meanwhile Bryn, Amanda, Sienna, and Devon all agreed that rental gowns would be shoddy and cheap as well as smelly. Abby kept her mouth closed as she watched in dismay.

"That's right!" Amanda exclaimed. "The dress I wore for the assembly stunk like BO."

"We'll make sure to smell our dresses before we rent them," Emma retorted.

"The money we save can be put toward Project Santa Sleigh," Felicia added.

Bryn rolled her eyes. "Well, you'll find me shopping for a lovely *non-smelly* formal on Saturday morning." She looked at the others. "You guys care to join me?" Amanda and Sienna quickly agreed, and now Bryn pointed at Abby. "What about you?" She frowned when Abby shook her head. "Please, don't tell me you're going to wear a rented gown too?"

Abby gave her an uneasy smile. "Actually, I promised my mom that I'd go dress shopping with her. Otherwise my dad won't pay for it. Not after the dress I got for the homecoming dance. Remember?"

"Hmm . . ." Bryn's forehead creased. "Well, I'd really hoped the DG could coordinate our dresses. You know, since the theme is red, white, and green. I was hoping we wouldn't all show up in the same color and—"

"Instead of focusing on our dresses, maybe we should focus on Project Santa Sleigh," Abby declared with irritation.

"Yeah!" Felicia eagerly agreed.

Bryn blinked. "There's plenty of time to do—"

"It's a little more than two weeks before the dance," Abby told her. "That means only two weekends, Bryn. That's *not* a whole lot of time."

"She's right," Emma added. "Felicia and the guys and I plan to get together this weekend to do something for our kids. We're taking this thing seriously."

"I plan on spending Saturday with Kent at the FAC," Abby told her. "What are you and Jason going to contribute?"

Bryn frowned. "Make the sleigh?"

Abby nodded briskly then stood. "Fine. Do that." As she walked away, she felt the resentment simmering inside of her. Why had she agreed to partner with Bryn? Never mind that they were supposed to be best friends. At least they used to be. Bryn was steadily becoming someone else . . . someone Abby didn't respect very much. The idea of being on a double date with Bryn and Jason—well, that was just too much!

• • ● • •

Cassidy hadn't really planned on getting her dress from the rental place, but it wasn't like she really cared either. After all, she'd never been very style conscious. Plus, like Felicia had pointed out, this would leave her more money to use for Project Santa Sleigh. All in all, it just made sense. She didn't mind that it had rubbed Bryn the wrong way either. In Cassidy's opinion, Bryn was getting a little too full of herself lately. Too obsessed with things like fashion, status, and money. Cassidy felt this was partly because of Amanda's influence and she still wished that they'd never allowed Amanda into the DG. Not that there was much to be done about that now. In all fairness, Sienna seemed pretty nice.

"Ready to shop till we drop?" Felicia said as they walked toward Cassidy's car in the school parking lot.

"Trust me, I'll be the first one to drop," Cassidy assured her. "Emma can attest to the fact that I'm not very good at this."

"For sure," Emma agreed a little too heartily. "Cassidy is probably the most fashion-challenged of the DG."

"You mean *before* I joined," Felicia said. "Never mind the fiasco I made of myself before Tristin made me into a total joke. I got rid of my, uh, *inappropriate* wardrobe, but I'm still not really getting it."

"Bryn's the fashionista," Cassidy told her. "She's the one who helped us with our makeovers."

"And Devon too," Emma added.

"Too bad Bryn didn't want to come with us," Felicia said.

"We should probably be relieved," Emma told her. "Bryn would probably just turn it into a big joke."

"Hang on." Cassidy held up her phone. "What about Devon?"

"She didn't want a rental dress," Emma reminded her.

"Yeah. But she might be willing to help us. I think she was getting a ride home with Amanda or Bryn."

"She probably wouldn't want them to know she was going with us," Emma pointed out.

"I'll figure out a way to get her to come." Cassidy hit Devon's number and quickly explained. "I need your expertise, Devon. You know how clueless I am about fashion."

"That's true. But . . ."

Cassidy knew that Devon was with the others and embarrassed to let on what she was considering. "Just tell them you're working with your partner—on something for the dance. That's true enough."

"Okay," Devon chirped. "Meet you at your car in a few minutes."

As Cassidy drove the four of them toward the strip mall, she wasn't sure whether Devon would be helpful or not. Based on some of Devon's sarcastic comments as she pulled into the parking lot, it seemed even more doubtful. But after they'd looked around the really huge store for just a few minutes, Devon started to change her tune.

"Some of these dresses are brand-new," she pointed out. "And there are some impressive names here too." She held up a dress. "Bryn loves this designer."

"Maybe you'll want to pick something out too," Cassidy encouraged her. "Save yourself a few bucks."

It took a couple of hours for them to make up their minds, but the money they were ultimately saving was well worth the time spent. Not only that, but the woman helping them also made sure that each dress would fit perfectly because the rental price included alterations.

"What a great place!" Felicia exclaimed as she gave a twirl in the sparkly red cocktail-length dress she'd chosen, making the skirt flare out prettily.

Cassidy gave her fitted emerald-green gown one last look in the mirror. "You guys really think this is okay?" she asked uncertainly. "This satiny fabric's not too over the top? The neck-line's not too low?"

"It's absolutely gorgeous on you," Emma assured her. "You'll knock Lane's eyeballs out."

"And that mint green is luscious on you," Felicia told Emma. "So soft and pretty."

"You think mint green is Christmassy enough?" Emma asked them.

"The dance is supposed to be red, white, and green," Cassidy told her. "That's mint *green*."

"The length is okay?" Emma asked. "I know Bryn and the others are probably going for floor-length gowns."

"I think you petite girls look better in the shorter dresses," the saleswoman assured Felicia and Emma. "You looked a bit buried in those longer gowns."

"I have to admit that all three of your dresses look really good," Devon told them. "No one would guess you'd rented them."

"What about you?" Cassidy asked. "That white sequined gown was pretty stunning."

"I don't look good in white."

"Is it the rental thing that's still bugging you?" Emma asked quietly.

Devon shrugged.

"You can always change your mind," Cassidy told her. "Sneak in here by yourself and rent a dress and no one has to even know about it." She laughed. "If that makes you feel better."

Devon wrinkled her nose, but Cassidy could tell she'd hit a nerve. Cassidy felt sorry for Devon. Her alliance with Bryn and the others could end up costing her, and Devon—perhaps even more than the others—probably couldn't afford to be extravagant.

Cassidy dropped Felicia and Emma at home first, then as she was driving Devon to Emma's grandmother's house, she reminded her about Project Santa Sleigh. "I've been making some lists and stuff. Lane and I plan to get together this weekend and get things rolling. Do you and Harris want to join us?"

"I promised Bryn I'd go shopping with her on Black Friday. Maybe on Saturday I can help. I'll text Harris and see what he's up to. And Grandma Betty has offered to help both me and Emma with some homemade jams and things to put in the sleigh."

"Speaking of the sleigh, we need to make a plan for that too."

"Let the guys handle it," Devon told her as Cassidy pulled into the driveway.

"I just want it to be nice," Cassidy said.

Devon made a sly grin. "You want to win?"

Cassidy shrugged. "I don't know. I'm not really into that red carpet stuff. But I'd like it to be nice for the kids."

"Well, I'd like it to be nice for them too. But now that I think about it, I wouldn't mind winning either." She winked. "Okay, I'll put my full effort into this, Cass. I promise."

"Maybe we can get together on Friday afternoon. After you're done shopping with Bryn and the others."

"It's a date." Devon made a finger wave then slammed the door.

Although it was somewhat reassuring that Devon seemed to care about Project Santa Sleigh and that she actually wanted to win, Cassidy wasn't convinced that she was going to make the best partner. She knew Devon didn't have the same level of enthusiasm that Emma had—for the kids. But maybe Cassidy could be a good influence on her.

• • ● • •

On the morning after Thanksgiving, Emma walked over to Felicia's house and together they rode the bus into the city, where they'd arranged to meet Isaac and Marcus at the Family Assistance Center. According to Abby, this was a great place to connect with needy kids. Kent had given Isaac a list of potential candidates. The plan was to select four children—one for each of them. What they would do after that was still something of a mystery, but at least they were getting started. After showing Helen at the front desk their IDs and release forms for the kids' parents plus the vouchers they'd gotten from school for this project, they filled out the visitors' information and were given name tags.

"Go ahead and make yourselves at home," Helen told them. "We encourage guests to participate in whatever activities interest them."

"I think we should all go our separate ways," Emma said as they studied the map of the building hanging by the front desk.

"I'm going to the gym," Marcus informed them.

"Me too," Isaac told him.

"I'm going to the arts and crafts room," Emma said.

"I'll check out the sewing center," Felicia proclaimed.

"Let's meet back at lunch," Marcus suggested as they parted ways.

Emma found her way to a rather dismal little room where an older woman named Diane was supervising arts and crafts.

She seemed unenthused and the kids, who did seem interested in doing something artsy, were restless. "Do you have a project for them to do?" Emma asked Diane.

"Not really," Diane admitted. "I usually just let them do what they like."

"Mind if I get involved?" Emma asked. "I love art."

Diane nodded eagerly. "Sure. I'd appreciate that."

Before long, Emma had a dozen kids making Christmas tree ornaments together, but it was a six-year-old girl named Mindy who really captured her attention. "You're an artist," Emma told Mindy as she watched her decorating a cardboard gingerbread man.

Mindy looked doubtful. "Really?"

"Absolutely." Emma pointed at Mindy's careful work. "That's beautiful."

Mindy gave her a cautious smile. "You like it?"

"I love it."

"Thanks." Mindy returned her attention to the glue she was using to draw a vest on the gingerbread man. Then she carefully sprinkled it with green glitter, shaking it onto the folded paper like Emma had shown them. "How's that?"

"Very elegant."

By lunchtime, Emma had made up her mind. If Mindy was interested and if her parents agreed, Emma would choose her.

As it turned out, they each found a child they wanted to help. Isaac had bonded with a seven-year-old boy named Jackson who loved playing basketball. Felicia and Marcus had picked twin siblings—six-year-old Rosa and Roberta Gonzales. With the help of Helen at the front desk, by the end of the day, all arrangements were made with the parents, and Isaac and Marcus offered Emma and Felicia a ride home.

"So what's next?" Emma asked as they got into Isaac's car.

"We should take the kids to do something fun," Marcus suggested. They kicked around various ideas, everything from seeing *The Nutcracker*, which the guys vetoed, to go-cart racing, which they decided was too old for these kids. They finally agreed on several things, including Christmas-gift shopping, a visit to Santa Village, lunch at a place with a kid-friendly environment, and a fun Christmas movie.

Emma knew some of these activities wouldn't be cheap, but she didn't want to put a damper on things by admitting that her budget might be a bit challenged. Plus, she knew there were available resources to help with some of these things. "What about the Christmas parade?" she asked. "It's tomorrow."

"Good idea," Felicia said eagerly. "And it's free."

"Speaking of that," Emma said carefully, "I want to contribute as much as I can to this project, but the truth is, I'm not exactly, uh, wealthy." She made a nervous laugh.

"That goes for me too," Felicia admitted.

"Maybe we should stop somewhere and have a kind of planning meeting," Marcus suggested. Because the guys were hungry and Marcus insisted on treating, they quickly agreed to have their meeting over burgers and shakes.

Emma offered to take notes for their ideas, and by the time they were finished with their food, they had scheduled a number of activities for the next two weekends, as well as a budget and a list of responsibilities for everyone. As it turned out, Isaac and Marcus wanted to cover most of the expenses, while Felicia and Emma helped to round up all the available free resources.

"With everyone doing their part, this should be a very cool Christmas for our kids," Isaac declared as they walked to his car.

"I'll borrow my mom's minivan to get the kids to the parade and everything tomorrow," Marcus told them.

"I'll do the phoning to set it up with their parents," Felicia offered.

"Maybe we should get the winter coats I told you about

before tomorrow's parade." Emma rubbed her hands together for warmth. "I heard it's going to get even colder and the kids might need them."

"Good idea," Marcus said. "We're not far from the police department you mentioned."

Isaac turned back toward the city, and before long they were sorting through an enormous pile of both new and "gently used" winter clothes that had been donated to the police department.

"Good thing you stopped when you did," a uniformed officer told them. "The rest of this is going to be dropped off for distribution after the Christmas parade."

It took about an hour for each of them to accumulate a set of coats, mittens, hats, boots, and other things for their Christmas kids. Emma couldn't wait to see Mindy's face when she presented her with the pink-and-purple jacket and matching hat and mittens. "Hey, we should take photos of the kids in their new stuff," she suggested as they loaded their loot in the trunk.

"Yeah," Marcus said eagerly. "Maybe we could put the pics in the sleigh, you know, to show that the kids really have them."

"Or we could make a video," Isaac suggested, "and put that in the sleigh."

"And give copies of it to the kids too," Felicia added.

"Hey, Isaac," Emma said. "Where are you going? You missed your—"

"That woman at the police station told me to swing by the fire department," Isaac told her. "They have Toys for Tots collected there, and if we show them our vouchers, we can get some things for the kids."

"Fantastic!" Felicia declared.

Just like at the police station, the fireman helping them explained that the remainder of the toys they'd collected would be distributed following tomorrow's parade. "I'm sure we'll collect more before Christmas," he assured them. "But you never know. Might be slim pickings by then. You kids are smart to get a head start on it." He grinned. "Nice to see teens taking an interest in something like this."

By the time they got back to the car, they were loaded down with all sorts of great stuff. And all of it was free! Emma could hardly believe it. As Isaac dropped her at home, she was even more determined to go over the list of resources that the school counselor had posted on the school's website. This was turning out to be even more fun than she'd expected. Sure, it was work too. But it was enjoyable work, and it was made much easier by everyone doing their part.

As Bryn stood in front of the full-length mirror on her closet door, she knew that this creamy white formal was absolutely gorgeous. From the structured, form-fitting strapless bodice down to the luminous pearly beadwork that glimmered like moonlight on the lower half of the skirt, everything about this gown was total perfection. With the right shoes and accessories, a sophisticated up-do for her hair, and a little tanning, she would definitely be the belle of the ball. Bryn gave a happy spin, watching as the weight of the beaded skirt made it swirl out slightly. Some three-inch heels would be perfect.

She gently removed the splendid gown, carefully hanging it back into the sleek Nordstrom's garment bag. It had been on sale, but it had not been cheap. Not by any means. Still, she assured herself, it was well worth it. If nothing else, it was already worth it just for the reaction she got from Amanda, Sienna, and Devon when she'd announced she was getting it. She knew they were not only surprised but understandably envious. Everyone had admired the gown on the rack, but Bryn had been the brave one who'd decided to try it on.

She hadn't told her parents how much it had cost yet, but it wasn't like Dad had really given her a limit. Oh, he'd warned her not to go overboard, but she would remind him that, as the chair of the Christmas ball, she was expected to wow everyone at the dance. And this gown was designed to do just that.

She couldn't wait to see Beth and Jack Hartford's faces when they saw her in it. For some reason that seemed almost more important to her than Jason's reaction. She did want Jason to be proud of her too, but the Hartfords were so rich . . . so influential . . . so supportive of this whole event. She really wanted to show them that she was something special. She wanted to impress them. Now if only she could find just the right shoes.

She went online, starting what would probably turn into an exhaustive search for the most chic pair of pearl-white shoes. Hopefully she'd find them for a good deal too. Dad would appreciate that. She'd just located a good possibility when she heard someone tapping on her door. Assuming it was Mom, she called out a distracted "come in," but it was Abby who entered her room.

"I texted and called you," Abby said a bit glumly as she peered over Bryn's shoulder.

"Check out these shoes." Bryn pointed to the photo. "Aren't they to die for?"

"They're okay, I guess."

"Well, wait until you see my dress." Bryn sprung to her feet, unzipping the garment bag to show Abby her fabulous find. "Did you ever see anything so beautiful?"

Abby's brow creased as she looked at the white gown. "Wow, it's really formal, isn't it?"

Bryn laughed as she extracted the dress. "Isn't it yummy?"

"I guess."

"What's up with you?" Bryn held the dress in front of her, dancing before the mirror again. "Why so gloomy?"

Abby frowned at Bryn. "I guess I'm worried about you."

"About me?" Bryn blinked in surprise. "Why? I'm doing just fine, Abby. You don't need to worry about me." She hung the dress back in the bag, carefully zipping it closed.

"Well, you and Jason are supposed to be our partners in Project Santa Sleigh," Abby began, "but it seems like you're more interested in things like your dress than you are in helping with it."

"I'm going to help with it," Bryn assured her. "Like I told you, I just wanted to get my dress figured out. That frees me up to focus on helping you." She pointed a finger at Abby. "Have you gotten your dress yet?"

Abby shook her head. "Mom and I are going shopping next week."

"Well, you don't want to put it off too long. Poor Sienna and Devon. They couldn't find a single thing today. Although Amanda got her dress too." Bryn gave her a smug smile. "Not as pretty as mine." She described it in detail to Abby. "To be honest, red is not Amanda's best color. Not that I mentioned that to her. She looked kind of washed out in it, though."

"Kent and I are going to FAC tomorrow. Do you want to come?"

"FAC?"

"Family Assistance Center."

"Oh." Bryn sat down to consider this. "Do I really need to go there? I mean, I want to help with these kids and everything, but is that the best use of my time?"

Abby scowled, making her face resemble an old lady's.

"It's just that I might be more useful doing things like shopping for the kids, you know? I'm such a good shopper. If you gave me the kids' sizes and stuff, I could probably put together some cool outfits." Bryn brightened. "Wouldn't that be fun? It could look really awesome in our sleigh. You know, to lay the clothes out with everything. Kind of like a store window. And we could prop some toys around and—"

"Wouldn't it be easier for you to pick things out for them if you knew them?"

"Tell me about them." Bryn waited.

"Well, Sarita is seven and Samuel is five."

"Wait." Bryn grabbed a pen and notepad from her desk. "What size do you think they wear?"

"I don't know. They seem about average size for their ages."

"The girl's seven and the boy's five?" Bryn asked.

"Yes."

"And what kind of coloring are they?" Bryn made notes.

"My kind of coloring," Abby said in a slightly chilly tone.

"Right." Bryn nodded. "They'll look great in bright, bold colors. This will be fun." She turned around to her computer and quickly pulled up some children's clothing websites. "What do you think of this?" She pointed to a sweater with big stripes of primary colors.

Abby leaned over to see it. "I guess that would be cute, but I'm not sure about sweaters. They might need stuff that's easier to wash, you know? Like things that are warm and sturdy."

"Still cute, though, right? I mean, just because kids are poor doesn't mean they can't look cute."

Abby's somber face cracked into a bit of a smile. "Yeah, Bryn, I guess being poor doesn't mean you can't have style."

"I can do my part by getting them some clothes?"

Abby let out a sigh. "Sure, why not."

"You don't sound very enthusiastic."

Abby patted Bryn on the back. "Look, Kent and I will be grateful for any help you and Jason can give. We just didn't like feeling like we were pulling this sleigh by ourselves. By the way, we got started on it and it's looking pretty good." Abby pulled out her phone and showed Bryn a photo of a cardboard structure that resembled a sporty-looking sleigh.

"Hey, that's not bad." Bryn nodded. "Maybe we could have a real chance to win this thing." Now she was imagining filling the sleigh with some pretty cool-looking stuff—maybe it could all be color coordinated. "What color do you plan to paint it?"

"We haven't decided."

"What if we kept everything in primary colors," Bryn suggested as she returned to her computer, switching over to toy websites and finding some sturdy-looking toys. "Like these. The sleigh could be red and blue and yellow." She pointed to a wooden puzzle. "And the clothes could be coordinated too. Can you imagine how cool that would look?"

"I guess." Abby cocked her head to one side. "But we want the stuff in the sleigh to be practical and enjoyable for the kids. Not just cool to look at. You know?"

"Look at these wooden puzzles. What kids wouldn't like them?"

"I don't know. Check the age range that the toys are made for. We want them to be appropriate for five- and seven-year-olds."

"I'm on it, Abby." Bryn clicked onto another site.

"Okay then. I better go because I'm on my bike and it'll be dark soon. I just wanted to make sure you were helping . . . that you're into this."

"Believe me, I'm into this." Bryn gave Abby a big, confident smile. "You're going to love what I bring to it. Who knows, it might be you and me doing the red carpet next year. Can you imagine?"

Abby shook her head. "Not really."

Bryn pointed to the bag hanging on her closet door. "I already have the perfect dress for it."

Abby laughed. "You're not going to be the star walking down

the red carpet, Bryn. Even if we won, we'd be sitting on the sidelines. Remember?"

"Who says we can't be shining like stars on the sidelines?"

Abby waved. "Good-bye, my delusional friend. Happy shopping."

• • • • •

The next week and a half passed in a crazy-busy blur for Abby. She was so glad that she'd quit the basketball team. Along with the demands of school and daily life, she was investing a lot of time on Project Santa Sleigh. Between doing things with young Sarita and Samuel, who had both become very special to her and Kent, she was also doing all she could to keep everyone else's enthusiasm for the project up. She continued to find and post new resources on the school's website, hoping to make quality gifts and goodies accessible to all. From what she was hearing, everyone in the school was really getting into the project. Whether it was for the kids or for the prizes was anyone's guess, but Abby didn't care—as long as it was a success. And she'd been thrilled to hear that the skating party was really going to happen. Scheduled for the Sunday afternoon after the dance, it was estimated that more than 130 children would be in attendance—with 78 filled sleighs awaiting them.

To Abby's pleasant surprise, Bryn had come through with flying colors on their sleigh too—well, sort of. She had certainly found a number of great bargains for the sleigh—all in the primary colors that she'd decided upon. Abby had to admit their stuff looked pretty stylish in the sleigh as the four of them admired their handiwork in Abby's garage on Thursday afternoon.

"I'll fluff it up with red, yellow, and blue tissue paper, and I'll have helium balloons in the same colors." Bryn beamed at them. "I think we could have a real good chance of winning."

"Wow." Jason poked Kent in the ribs. "Imagine you and me at the Rose Bowl, bro."

"Two days until the big night." Bryn eagerly rubbed her hands together. "I can't wait."

"What I'm really looking forward to is the skating party," Abby admitted. "I can't wait to see the looks on the kids' faces. Not just our kids either. All of them. It's going to be awesome."

"Speaking of awesome," Bryn said to Abby, "are you going to let me see your dress?"

Kent elbowed Jason. "I think that's girl-speak for 'time to split.'"

After the guys left, Abby led Bryn up to her room. She was pretty sure that Bryn wouldn't be overly impressed with the formal she'd chosen. "I wanted to be frugal," she explained as she opened her closet.

"Don't tell me you went to the rental place too!"

"I thought about it. But Mom and I went to Dress 4 Less and they had a markdown rack that—"

"Dress 4 Less? Markdown rack?" Bryn gasped dramatically as she collapsed onto Abby's bed. "Tell me it ain't so."

Abby removed the cranberry-colored cocktail-length dress and held it up to her. She actually kind of liked it and could almost imagine wearing it more than once.

"It's short," Bryn exclaimed.

"Yeah. But some girls are wearing short dresses. Emma's is short and—"

"But mine is floor length," Bryn said. "You saw it—remember?"

"I know. That doesn't mean I have to—"

"But I wanted us to look good together."

"We will look good. We'll be red and white—very Christmassy."

Bryn just shook her head. As Abby looked at her image in the mirror, she was pleased with her choice. Not only did it look good, it would be comfortable too. "My shoes are really cool," she told Bryn. "I think you'll like them." Bryn approved of the glitzy silver-heeled sandals, but she was not a fan of the dress. As Abby told her good-bye, she realized that she really didn't care. Bryn might be a fashionista, but she wasn't Abby's boss.

* ● ● ● *

Cassidy could tell that something was wrong as she walked across the cafeteria toward her friends. Bryn looked seriously angry, and Amanda looked curiously smug. "What's up?" Cassidy asked as she set down her tray.

"Amanda went over my head," Bryn exclaimed hotly. "She went to Mr. Worthington and together they made the executive decision that the chairs of the dance committees will not be allowed to participate in Project Santa Sleigh!"

"That's not exactly right," Abby corrected. "We *can* participate. We just can't be in the competition."

"So our team—Abby and Kent and Jason and me—we don't even have a chance at winning." Bryn scowled at Amanda.

"Same with us," Amanda said lightly.

"Well, you didn't even have a chance at winning in the first place," Bryn snapped at her. "I saw your sleigh and it's nothing like what we—"

"How did you see our sleigh?" Amanda demanded.

"Jason got a picture of it from Darrell and—"

"It's supposed to be top secret," Amanda said hotly.

"What does it matter now?" Sienna said calmly. "Why not just let it go?"

But the debate was on, and Amanda and Bryn didn't seem willing to let it rest. Finally it was Devon who got them to settle down. "I thought we were doing this for the kids," she said loudly. "*Remember?* It's about the kids. It's Christmas and peace on earth and goodwill toward men. Remember *Christmas*?"

Cassidy felt strangely proud of Devon just then—and glad that they were partnered in this after all. She also felt a slight surge of hope that they might have a real chance at winning this contest, because their sleigh was looking pretty good.

"Devon's right," Abby chimed in. "This is supposed to be about the kids. The prizes were just a way to get everyone on board. I'm out of the competition too, and even though I've worked hard on Project Santa Sleigh, I don't even care that I can't win. The best part of all this will be seeing the kids' faces on Sunday." She pointed to Amanda and Bryn. "And besides, we get to be judges. That'll be fun."

Bryn just rolled her eyes.

"So the chairs are the judges?" Cassidy asked with some concern. "Is that fair? Can you guys really be unbiased when it comes to your friends?"

"We're not the only judges," Bryn explained grimly. "Jack and Beth Hartford are judging, along with Mr. Worthington and Mrs. Dorman and three other teachers. Ten in all. We have evaluation forms and we'll rank the entries with numbers. It's all very official—and fair." She frowned. "Except that we can't be in the competition."

"And we have to go to the dance early to do the judging," Amanda added. "I hadn't really counted on that."

All in all it seemed fair to Cassidy. And if it increased her team's odds of winning . . . well, she wouldn't complain.

As Devon waited for Cassidy to zip up the back of her gown, she was uncertain. "Do you think this color of red works for me?" she asked Cassidy. She'd gone to Cass's house to get dressed, and the boys would be picking them up soon. "With my auburn hair I have to be careful. It seemed okay at the rental shop, but in this light I'm not so sure."

"There," Cassidy told her. "See for yourself."

Devon turned around and peered in Cassidy's full-length mirror. The long, fitted gown was made of a dark burgundy velvet, and seeing it with her hair, she realized that it was actually kind of nice.

"You look gorgeous." Cassidy stepped next to her. "With me in my emerald and you in your burgundy, well, we look downright festive."

Devon laughed. "We really do."

As promised, Devon helped Cassidy with her hair and makeup. They were just finishing up when Cass's mom called up the stairs to say the boys had arrived. "Ready for this?" Cassidy asked with a nervous expression.

"Sure. Why not?" Together they strolled down the stairs like they were princesses, and the looks on Lane's and Harris's faces seemed like a pretty good payoff. Devon was sure that no one—besides her friends—would guess that the gown had been rented. And no one, except maybe Bryn, would remember that she was wearing the same shoes from the homecoming dance.

Everyone, including Cassidy's parents, pulled out their phones and started snapping photos. Like Devon had promised, she sent hers to Grandma Betty. And then, feeling surprisingly generous, she sent one to her mom. Not that she probably cared, since she was still treating Devon like an orphan.

"Did you get our sleigh there all right?" Cassidy asked Lane. "By the five o'clock deadline and without anything falling apart?"

"Yeah. You should see that place with all those sleighs! Pretty cool." Lane held up a ticket. "And here's our admission."

"The sleds are all circled around the ballroom like it's a race-track," Harris told them. "Kinda like the Santa Indy 500."

"Were the judges there yet?" Devon asked.

"I don't know," Harris told her. "But you can bet they've been there by now."

"Do you think we have a chance to win?" Cassidy asked the guys. "How did we compare with the others?"

"Hard to say," Harris admitted.

"Let's go," Devon said eagerly. "I want to see this."

Because Harris had driven tonight, Devon waited for him to open the passenger door for her, feeling slightly like royalty when she slid into the front seat. Already this was going far better than her previous two dates. Perhaps she had actually learned something from those disaster evenings. Perhaps she was growing up.

Because so many of the kids had exhausted their finances in putting together the Santa sleighs, everyone had pretty much agreed to forgo eating out before the dance tonight. This suited Devon just fine, because she was always too nervous to eat much before a dance anyway. The soup that Cass's mom had made for them had been just about perfect.

Harris pulled up to valet parking and soon they were all out and strolling into the dance. As Devon considered the effort that the four of them had put into Project Santa Sleigh and the way this date had all fallen into place, she felt incredibly good. Like this was the way it was done. Even if their sleigh didn't win tonight—although she felt they had a chance—she would go home feeling like a winner. She just knew it.

• • • • •

Bryn had been pretty impressed and amazed at the Santa Sleigh entries. To be perfectly honest, it seemed that many of them outshone her team's efforts. She could tell that Abby thought so too. Maybe it really was better to be out of the competition. At least she wouldn't have to admit that they'd lost.

The sleighs were numbered, and the team of judges was about halfway around the room when they stopped at a sleigh she actually recognized. The one that Emma had made for the assembly. As Bryn studied it, she felt slightly disappointed. Oh, the sleigh itself was still colorful and fun, but the toys and wrapped presents inside of it seemed rather miserly and somewhat anticlimactic. Especially compared with the other entries. Although there was a small flat-screen TV wedged into the back of it. But was that an appropriate gift for young children? "This one seems a bit dull," she said aloud.

"Don't be too quick," Jack told her. "See this?" He picked up a remote with a note that said "Click me." He pushed the button, then called the other judges to gather around to see. Together they watched a video where four adorable little kids were doing all sorts of fun things. To start with, the kids were trying on colorful new winter wear, and then they were watching a Christmas parade. Sometimes the teens were in the footage with the kids, but someone had edited to be sure their faces were obscured. Mostly it was just film of the kids. The next scene was the kids wobbling around on the same ice-skating rink where tomorrow's party would be held. The legs of the teens showed as they helped the kids practicing some skating skills. This was followed by a lunch scene, and after that the kids played miniature golf and even went bowling. There were spots of the kids going shopping for Christmas gifts for their family members and shots of them wrapping the presents afterwards. Next they were filmed at a tree lot, where they picked out Christmas trees and then took them to their houses to decorate. There was footage of the four smiling faces waiting in line for a new Christmas movie and eating pizza afterwards. Finally they saw shots of the kids in their homes, proudly presenting food boxes and gift certificates to the surprised parents.

"Wow," Jack said when he finally clicked it off. *"Impressive."*

"Those kids really put a lot of thought and effort into their project," Mrs. Dorman commented.

"And they invested a lot of themselves in it too." Beth bent down to make notes on her list.

"That took some serious time and energy," Mr. Worthington added.

Some of the other judges made similar comments, and eventually the team of judges continued on their way. As Bryn wrote down numbers for the other entries, some that were full of toys and looked flashy and colorful and charming, she couldn't get that video out of her head. Emma and her team had really done it right.

It took nearly two hours to judge all the sleighs, but Bryn's mind was already made up, and as she handed her sheet to Jack, she suspected she wasn't the only one who'd felt this way. At least she hoped she wasn't. In her opinion, if anyone truly deserved to win, it was Emma, Felicia, Isaac, and Marcus.

"Meet you back down here in a few minutes?" Jason asked as she, Abby, and Amanda were exiting the ballroom. Jack and Beth had offered the girls the use of their hotel suite to get ready.

"A few minutes?" Bryn frowned. "Is that all we have?"

"It's almost 7:00," he pointed out.

"Well, we might just be elegantly late," she retorted.

As she rode the elevator with Abby and Amanda, she asked what they thought about the sleighs. "Did any of them stand out to you?"

"Sure," Abby said. "One in particular—and not just because they're friends either."

"Emma and Felicia got my vote," Bryn confessed.

"I picked them too," Amanda admitted.

"Wouldn't that be cool if they won," Abby said as they hurried down the hall to the suite the Hartfords' had offered to share with them.

Because they'd already done their hair and makeup, it didn't take long to dress, but when Bryn stepped out in her long white gown, Abby frowned ever so slightly. "What's wrong?" Bryn asked her.

"Nothing," Abby said quickly.

Amanda was starting to giggle.

"What is it?" Bryn looked over her shoulder, trying to see the back of her dress. "Do I have a price tag hanging somewhere?"

"No, nothing like that." Abby was giggling now too.

"What's going on?" Bryn demanded.

"Nothing." Abby tugged on Bryn's arm. "Let's go. It's almost 7:30, and I want to be there when they announce the winner."

Yet it was obvious that both Abby and Amanda were amused by something as they rode down the elevator. When it stopped at the lobby, Bryn pushed the Close button on the elevator panel.

"I refuse to let you guys out until you tell me what's so funny," she told them.

Abby and Amanda exchanged amused looks, then turned back to Bryn. "It's just that . . ." Abby laughed nervously. "You sort of look like . . . well, like . . ."

"Like you're getting married," Amanda finished for her.

"Yeah," Abby said. "Is that a bridal gown?"

"What?" Bryn tried to peer at her reflection in the smoky mirrored wall inside the elevator. "A bride? Seriously?"

"Yeah, but you're a really pretty one," Abby said as the door opened.

"I look like a bride?" Bryn repeated in a horrified voice as they exited the elevator. *"Really?"*

As Jason walked up to meet her, she could see that he had a slightly puzzled expression, which he quickly turned into a grin. "Don't you look pretty!" He handed her a box with a red-and-white wrist corsage.

"Amanda and Abby think I look like a bride," she hissed at him.

He laughed. "Well, I can kinda understand that."

"Come on," Abby called to Bryn. "Kent says they're about to announce the winners. Don't you want to hear it?"

All Bryn could think about was that everyone thought she looked like a bride. She'd wanted to be the belle of the ball—not a bride! As they walked into the ballroom, it all flashed through her mind—all the time and effort she'd put into her appearance, how she'd carefully picked everything out, how she'd spared no expense, how her dad had hit the roof when he'd seen the bill. All for what?

● ● ● ● ●

Emma was so excited that it almost felt like she was floating as she and Isaac and Felicia and Marcus walked into the ballroom. She felt pretty in her rented mint-green dress and thrift store shoes, and Isaac looked and acted like a real gentleman in his rented tux. This was going to be fun!

"Look at all these sleighs!" she exclaimed as they walked the perimeters of the ballroom. "Do you guys realize how many kids' lives are going to be touched by this?"

"I can't wait to see everyone at the ice-skating rink tomorrow," Felicia said. "I even have a few more things to add to our sleigh."

"Wow, some of these sleighs are really something." Marcus pointed to one that was heaped high.

"Ours looks a little empty in comparison," Emma said as they came to it.

"But that was the plan," Isaac quietly reminded her.

A small crowd of onlookers was watching the video with interest.

"Looks like it's doing just what we hoped it would do," Marcus pointed out.

"Anyway, the kids sure had fun," Felicia added. They continued on around the circle, checking out all of the competition.

"I didn't know we had so much creativity at our school," Emma admitted after they made the complete circle. "People really worked hard on this."

Mr. Worthington was trying to get everyone's attention up in front, announcing that they were getting ready to reveal the winners of Project Santa Sleigh. "To do this, I'd like to invite the chairs of the committee up here." Emma watched as Bryn, escorted by Jason and trailed by Amanda and Abby, got onto the small stage.

"It looks like a wedding," Isaac whispered to her.

Emma laughed. "I was just thinking the same thing."

Bryn took the microphone from Mr. Worthington. Emma could tell she wasn't exactly comfortable in her long white gown, which did seem rather wedding-like. But she graciously thanked everyone for coming, making a sweet little speech about the enthusiastic participation in the contest. Finally she handed the mike to Jason.

He held up an envelope. "This, my friends, contains the winning entry—the four lucky people who will win the grand prize of Rose Bowl and red carpet tickets." He waved it in the air. "You guys ready?"

Everyone cheered and he slowly opened the envelope. "The winning sleigh is number 37, and it was put together by Emma Parks and Isaac—" But that was all that Emma could hear because everyone was clapping and cheering. Isaac swooped her into a lifted hug, and then the four friends did a group hug. Finally they went up to the stage to claim their prize. Emma didn't think she'd ever had a happier moment.

The celebration got even better when, later on, she was congratulated by all her friends in the DG. Every single one of them seemed genuinely happy for her and for Felicia too. As they were all gathered around the table, chattering happily together, Emma realized that the DG had grown—not just in numbers but as people too.

Santa Comes Early at Northwood Academy

Tuesday, December 16

Christmas showed up early for 137 appreciative children on Sunday afternoon. At Ice Capers skating rink, a magical Christmas extravaganza was hosted by students from Northwood Academy. Children and their families were presented with 78 wildly decorated sleighs, constructed by these motivated high school students and filled with all the wonders of the season. Spirits were high as children skated with their teen benefactors, visited with Santa Claus, and snacked on treats.

How did Northwood Academy get so many students involved in such a generous project? A contest. The winners of this contest, called Project Santa Sleigh, produced a charming video showing how they'd spent time and energy with four deserving children. Their prize: tickets to the Rose Bowl and to the Oscars red carpet. But according to Emma Parks, one of the winners, they would've gladly done it anyway. "It was so much fun," she said as she paused from skating with her young friend Mindy. "It really is better to give than receive."

The Project Santa Sleigh video is available on YouTube, where we've heard it's already going viral. Hopefully generosity and benevolence will too.

KEEP READING
for a sneak peek of
The Dating Games #4:
PROM DATE

'm so envious, I could spit," Bryn declared.

"Just don't spit in here, okay?" Emma teased. The six Dating Games friends were seated at a big corner table in the airport restaurant, waiting for their pizza to be served. It was the last Friday in February, and the plan for the afternoon, arranged by Cassidy, was to give Emma and Felicia—the winners of the Project Santa Sleigh competition—a nice little send-off party before they boarded the nonstop jet to Los Angeles. Emma was so excited that she wasn't even sure she could eat a whole slice of pizza, but she would at least pretend to enjoy it. Mostly she was just happy to be here with her friends. "Honestly," she told Bryn, "I wish you *could* go. I wish you all could go."

"Well, I'd give anything to be in your shoes," Bryn confessed.

"Really?" Felicia's dark eyes twinkled as she stuck out a foot. "You like these flip-flops, do you? Wanna trade?"

"Or maybe these?" Emma held up a foot. She knew that Bryn wouldn't be caught dead in her practical walking sandals.

Bryn gave them both a tolerant smile. "Well, I didn't mean

literally. But I have been wondering why I didn't try harder to win the Project Santa Sleigh contest myself."

"Like that was going to happen," Abby taunted. "Get real."

"But the red carpet! At only the biggest celebrity event of the year—*the Oscars*!" Bryn moaned dramatically as she pointed at Emma and Felicia. "And you two aren't even *into* fashion."

"Thanks a lot." Emma feigned offense.

"Sorry." Bryn looked slightly contrite. "That was my jealousy talking."

Emma gave her a sympathetic smile. It was ironic that someone like Bryn could be jealous of Emma and Felicia.

"It's okay," Felicia told Bryn. "Everyone knows that I'm seriously fashion challenged. If you hadn't helped me pack yesterday, I'd probably look like a total loser down in LA this weekend."

"I'm not trying to be mean." Bryn sounded like she was backpedaling now. "But you guys know me—I'm the one who obsesses over fashion and style and all that 'shallow' stuff." She rolled her big blue eyes.

Emma chuckled, remembering Bryn's New Year's resolution less than two months ago. Bryn had resolved to stop being so superficial, but she obviously still had a long road ahead. Who could blame her for feeling bummed, though? Winning this amazing trip to Hollywood had pretty much blown Emma's mind. She still could barely believe they were really going.

"Excuse me, Bryn," Abby interjected. "I might not be an obsessed fashionista like you, but I happen to care about style, thank you very much. I feel a little bummed about not going too."

"What about me when it comes to appearances?" Devon demanded. "I'm not exactly slumming here." She held her head higher, pausing to pat her auburn curls. "I care about my looks too."

"Hey, ladies, we're not here to argue over fashion." Cassidy picked up her soda, lifting it high for a toast. "We're here to celebrate Emma and Felicia. Here's to them having a great trip to Los Angeles and a fabulous time at the red carpet event." Everyone lifted their glasses, clinking them together and adding individual toasts, which went from serious to silly, until all six of them were giggling.

"You guys are so lucky." Devon playfully punched Emma in the shoulder.

"Luck had nothing to do with it," Cassidy defended. "Emma and Felicia worked hard to win the contest—fair and square."

"That's true," Abby agreed.

"But the kids we helped were the real winners," Felicia said humbly. "Rosa and Roberta and Mindy and Jackson—the best part of that whole project was seeing their faces light up every time we did something with them. That in itself would've been enough of a reward for me."

"Which reminds me, I promised to send the kids photos from the red carpet—just like Isaac and Marcus did from the Rose Bowl." Emma double-checked to make sure her she'd put the Family Assistance Center's phone number in the iPhone that Isaac had insisted she borrow. So sweet of him!

"Don't forget to send us photos too," Bryn reminded her.

"Yeah," Devon agreed. "I want the whole trip documented, from beginning to end, so it feels like we're there with you."

"We've already told you a dozen times that we'll keep you posted," Emma reassured her.

"Emma and I have it all worked out," Felicia added. "She'll be the photographer and I'll be the texter. Between the two of us, you should have pretty good coverage. Anything beyond that, and you better just turn on your televisions or watch a live stream."

"Don't forget to snag some selfies," Devon insisted. "We want to see you actually rubbing elbows with celebs—you know, to prove you were really there."

Bryn set her drink down with a dreamy look in her eyes. "I wonder if you'll see Taylor Lautner."

Emma wrinkled her nose. "Seriously? You're still into him? I thought he was, like, *so last year*."

Cassidy laughed loudly as she gave Emma a high five. "Good one."

"Anyway, we'll do our best," Emma reassured Bryn. "And if I happen to see Taylor, I'll set my personal bias aside and grab a pic. Want me to blow him a kiss from you too?"

Bryn frowned at Emma. "Funny."

They continued to laugh and joke until their pizza arrived, and as Emma looked around the table, she couldn't help but be thankful for this group of good friends. It seemed slightly ironic that the Dating Games, a club they'd created to improve their dating life, had brought them closer together as friends. During the past six months their friendships had become more important than dating. Not that Emma cared to admit this out loud.

"I'm so glad you guys came to the airport to see us off," Emma told them as they were finishing up. "It's been great."

Cassidy held up her arm, pointing to her watch. "Speaking of seeing you off, you promised your mom you'd meet her at security by 5:45. That's like right now."

Emma nodded. "Yeah, but our flight's not until—"

"Boarding time is 6:10." Felicia reached for her bag. "And our gate's in another terminal. Plus security might be busy since it's a Friday. We better go."

Devon blinked. "You sound like you've done this before."

"Lots of times," Felicia told her. "We visit relatives in California about once a year."

"Well, you guys better get moving," Bryn said.

Emma opened her purse, reaching for some money.

"The pizza is on us," Cassidy told her. "Save your money for LA."

All the girls stood, and everyone took turns hugging Felicia and Emma good-bye—acting as if they were going around the world.

"How long are your friends going to be gone?" the waitress asked Cassidy with concerned eyes.

"Just until Monday," Cassidy said brightly.

The waitress chuckled and walked away.

Emma and Felicia waved their last good-byes and hurried on down toward the security lines with their purses and carry-on bags in tow. Emma hadn't been overly thrilled that her mother was going with them as an escort, but because Felicia's parents refused to let their daughter take this trip without an adult along, Emma had agreed. Even though it meant she and Felicia had to exchange their first-class tickets for coach to cover Emma's mom's airfare, everyone had agreed it was well worth it in the end.

Really, it was better than having Felicia's overprotective mom along with them. Fortunately, she had to stay home with her other two children. The upside of this arrangement was that Emma's mom was a lot more laid-back than Felicia's parents.

"There's my mom up there." Emma pointed to where her mom was standing near the end of the security line—a cup of coffee in one hand and her phone in the other.

"I was just about to call you," Mom told Emma as they all got into line together.

"Sorry, we lost track of the time," Emma told her.

"Luckily the line hasn't been very long." Mom tossed the remains of her coffee in the trash container and sighed. "So, girls, *are we having fun yet*?"

Emma made a face, and Felicia just laughed.

"I feel a tiny bit bad that my ticket ousted you two from your first-class seats." Emma's mom made a slight smirk. "Or not."

"You're so funny," Felicia told her. "I'm glad you're going with us, Mrs. Parks."

"I'm glad too." Emma's mom nodded eagerly. "I'd be even more glad if I got to go to the red carpet event with you as well. But I guess you can't have everything." She patted Felicia on the back. "Just to make this trip more fun for all of us, you can't keep calling me Mrs. Parks. Okay?"

Felicia looked slightly uneasy.

"Please, just call me Susan."

Felicia nodded. "Okay. Susan."

"Even though I'm here to make sure you two darlings don't get into any trouble, let's just pretend that we're three girls out to have a good time."

Emma refrained from rolling her eyes.

"Hey, it could be worse," her mom reminded her.

Emma smiled. That was actually true. What if Emma's mom was like Devon's mom—a wild and crazy partier who took up with strange men? Now that would be scary. Or her mom could be like Felicia's mom, fretting over everything and insisting that her little girl dress like an eight year old. "I'm glad you came too," Emma quietly told her mom as they moved forward in the line.

Mom smiled at her, gently patting her on the back. "I'll try not to embarrass you . . . too much."

"Hey, I just got a text from Marcus." Felicia turned to Emma, holding up her phone. "He and Isaac are parked on the other side of the river, straight across from the airport. They want to watch as our plane takes off. Isn't that sweet?"

"Seriously?" Emma blinked in surprise. Although they'd gone out a few times and she did really like him, Isaac really wasn't her "boyfriend" per se. For him and Marcus to go to this much trouble . . . well, it really was sweet.

"Yeah. Marcus wants to know which side of the plane we're seated on. He wants us to look down while they wave at us from below."

"I think I printed out the seating chart of the plane." Mom

fished in her oversized travel bag, pulling out the packet she'd carefully prepared for them a few weeks ago, and sure enough, she had plane-shaped map. She pointed to a spot. "We're pretty far back. It looks like you girls are on the left, and I'm on the right."

"Great." Felicia nodded as she texted back to Marcus.

"We'll take a selfie to send them once we're seated," Emma told Felicia as they moved forward in the security line. "Tell them to send us one of them down by the river too."

"Good idea." Felicia turned back to her phone. "This is so fun."

"I know." Emma grinned. "Remember how they sent photos and texts to us from their Rose Bowl trip? Acting like they were such superstars. Now we can do the same thing back to them. Cool."

They had reached the first TSA agent, and although Mom and Felicia were ahead of her, Emma realized she needed to get out her ID and boarding pass. She found a rumpled boarding pass, but as she fumbled through her purse for her driver's license, the man in a dark uniform waited with a grim expression.

"I know I have it," Emma nervously assured him as she tore through her previously organized purse, spilling a couple of items onto the floor. She knelt down, gathering up a hairbrush and lip gloss and continuing to dig through her now messy bag. "I'm sorry it's taking so long."

The security guard said nothing, just bounced his pen up and down with what seemed aggravated impatience.

"Oh, here it is." Emma held up her license with a nervous smile. "You don't have to send me back home after all." Ignoring her attempt at humor, he simply studied her ID and boarding pass, frowning intently as if he thought she was carrying weapons of mass destruction in the soles of her sandals.

Suddenly Emma felt extremely uneasy. What if she blew this?

What if they did a complete body search and made her miss the plane? Because it was her first flight—and her first time through airport security—her friends had warned her to be careful. Okay, some of it was just good-natured teasing, but some of it was actual advice. Emma was well aware that things could turn ugly if you did something wrong. Like you weren't supposed to joke with the security dudes, particularly about having weapons or explosives. Not funny. You also didn't argue with them even if you thought they were being unreasonable or stupid. But as she waited for the grumpy-looking man to return her ID and boarding pass, she could feel herself literally starting to sweat.

Fortunately, she was allowed to move on, but now it was time to dig her Ziploc baggie of toiletries from her purse, load her stuff into a plastic tub, and hoist her carry-on onto the conveyor for the X-ray machine. As Emma fumbled with these tasks, not sure which one to do first, she felt a panic attack coming on. Mom was about to walk through the X-ray machine, but Felicia paused from preparing her own baggage, insisting that Emma go first. Felicia grabbed Emma's bag and stuff and set it ahead of her own things, coaching Emma as they went.

"It's her first time flying," Felicia explained to a TSA agent. "She's kinda nervous."

"Oh, well, it's not too painful." The woman smiled at Emma. "Now just step up to that line there and wait until I wave you on through the X-ray. Don't worry, we don't bite."

Emma's mouth felt dry as she followed the directions. She stood with her toes on the line, trying not to freak over the idea of being X-rayed—was it really like Devon had said? Did they actually see you naked? Eventually the woman waved her through.

"Stop and put your feet right on those footprints," she told Emma. "Hold very still and place your hands over your head like this." She demonstrated. Emma followed her example, holding

Melody Carlson

her breath as she waited for the machine to do its thing, and then the woman waved her on out. Feeling somewhat relieved but still flustered, Emma went over to the other side, watching as Felicia calmly went through the same process.

Finally, they were both gathering their bags and things, hurrying to get out of the way of others now coming through. Felicia made sure that Emma got everything, including the Ziploc bag that she nearly left behind.

"See, that wasn't so bad," Felicia said cheerfully.

"Thanks to you for helping me." Emma felt relieved to exit the security area, scanning the terminal for her mom and spying her over by a nearby set of benches. "That was much more stressful than I expected."

"Yeah." Felicia slowly wheeled both their carry-on bags as Emma attempted to stuff her toiletries back into her purse, adjusting the purse strap which seemed to have come undone in the X-ray. "You reminded me of my little sister," Felicia said quietly. "Sofia always gets flustered going through security. I try to help her too." Felicia's dark eyes turned unexpectedly sad.

"Are you missing your family?" Emma took her carry-on bag from Felicia, studying her friend's expression and hoping that she wasn't the homesick type. Emma realized how close Felicia was with her family, but what if she regretted taking this trip?

"No . . . no, that's not it. Not exactly anyway." Felicia's brow creased and her lower lip quivered slightly, almost as if she was on the verge of tears.

"What's wrong then?" Emma pulled Felicia aside, looking into her eyes. "I can tell you're upset about something."

"I didn't want to say anything about it, Emma. Didn't want to spoil our trip."

"What is it?" Emma demanded. "You have to tell me."

"It's just that I'm worried about Sofia." Felicia sighed deeply. "It's silly, really."

"You mean because Sofia's been sick?" Emma knew that Felicia's little sister had gone through some bad bouts of flu this past winter.

"Yeah . . . She had some tests earlier this week." Felicia lowered her voice. "For leukemia."

"Leukemia?" Emma tried to take this in. "Really?"

Felicia attempted a half smile. "I'm sure the results will be just fine. They were supposed to come back this afternoon, but Mom didn't hear back yet. I really shouldn't have mentioned it, Emma. Not right before our big trip. The only reason they tested her was just to rule it out."

"You were right to tell me." Emma placed a hand on Felicia's shoulder. "Of course Sofia will be fine. She's just had some stubborn bugs, that's all. I heard this was a bad year for the flu."

"Yeah." Felicia nodded. "That's what my parents keep saying too."

"But I'll be praying for Sofia just the same," Emma promised. "For her to get completely well." As they rejoined Emma's mom, Emma knew that she would keep this promise. She would pray for her friend's eight-year-old sister. Even though she felt certain that sweet little Sofia couldn't possibly have a sickness as serious as leukemia, she also knew that Sofia had missed a fair amount of school this winter. It was high time for Felicia's little sister to get well.

Melody Carlson is the award-winning author of over two hundred books, including *The Jerk Magnet*, *The Best Friend*, *The Prom Queen*, *Double Take*, and the Diary of a Teenage Girl series. Melody recently received a *Romantic Times* Career Achievement Award in the inspirational market for her books. She and her husband live in central Oregon. For more information about Melody, visit her website at www.melodycarlson.com.

Meet Melody at
MelodyCarlson.com

....

- Enter a contest for a signed book
- Read her monthly newsletter
- Find a special page for book clubs
- Discover more books by Melody

Become a fan on Facebook

f Melody Carlson Books

"Forget about The Hunger Games!
The Dating Games #1: First Date,
by Melody Carlson, is the new series to which
you should be drawn."

—TheCelebrityCafe.com

Hidden Identities, Colliding Cultures, and Miscommunication Combine for an Entertaining Read

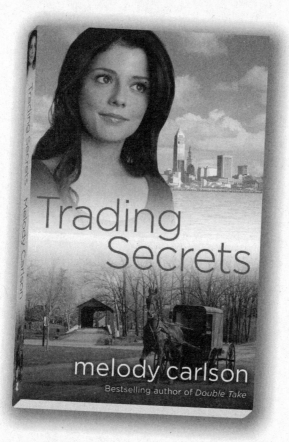

Micah and her Amish pen pal Zach have been trading secrets since fifth grade. Now that they plan to meet face-to-face, she'll have to admit the one secret she's never shared.

Shannon's summer just got a whole lot more
. . . AMISH?

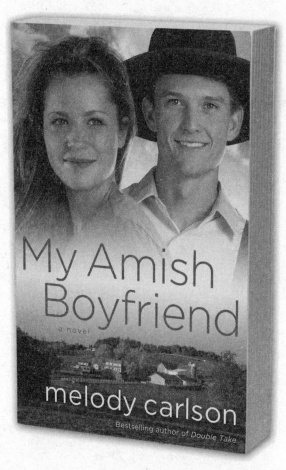

"Carlson hits all the right notes
in this wonderful story that grips you from
the beginning and does not let go."

—RT Book Reviews, ★★★★⯪ TOP PICK!

Katrina Yoder has the voice of an angel, but her Amish
parents believe singing is prideful vanity. When she wins a
ticket to sing in Hollywood, her life is turned upside down.

Revell
a division of Baker Publishing Group
www.RevellBooks.com